A VOYAGER IS IN DANGER

I have been alerted to the situation with Piper. It was a dirty trick, but you must stay strong. There is a bigger task at hand. The future of Earth depends on Team Alpha.

On Tundra, you will face an ice age. If you fail, we could soon be facing an ice age here on Earth. There is no time for distractions. We will get Piper back in due time. For now, please review the ZRK probe reports and prepare to enter a deep freeze.

P9-AZW-960

Shawn Phillips

Shawn Phillips

Commanding Officer | Voyagers Program | Base Ten

Life can't survive at extreme temperatures. . . .

But on this frozen planet, a creature is thriving.
And it's hungry.

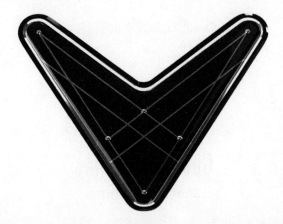

ESCAPE THE VORTEX

Don't miss a single Voyage. . . .

(1) **Project Alpha**
D. J. MacHale

(2) **Game of Flames**
Robin Wasserman

(3) **Omega Rising**
Patrick Carman

(4) **Infinity Riders**
Kekla Magoon

(5) **Escape the Vortex**
Jeanne DuPrau

Coming Soon:

(6) **The Seventh Element**
Wendy Mass

5

VOYAGERS

ESCAPE THE VORTEX

Jeanne DuPrau

Random House New York

Copyright © 2016 by PC Studios Inc.
Full-color interior art, puzzles, and codes copyright © Animal Repair Shop
Voyagers digital and gaming experience by Animal Repair Shop

All rights reserved. Published in the United States by Random House
Children's Books, a division of Penguin Random House LLC, New York.

Random House and the colophon are registered trademarks of
Penguin Random House LLC.

Visit us on the Web! randomhousekids.com

Educators and librarians, for a variety of teaching tools, visit us at
RHTeachersLibrarians.com

VoyagersHQ.com

Library of Congress Cataloging-in-Publication Data
is available upon request.
ISBN 978-0-385-38670-8 (trade) | ISBN 978-0-385-38672-2 (lib. bdg.) |
ISBN 978-0-385-386871-5 (ebook)

Printed in the United States of America
10 9 8 7 6 5 4 3 2 1
First Edition

ESCAPE THE VORTEX

1

Piper Williams hovered in her air chair up by the ceiling of her prison—the *Light Blade*'s training room. She'd been locked in here for weeks now, with only the robot SUMI for company. It was *way* too long. She was bored, she was furious, and—she had to admit it—she was desperate. If she was ever going to see her own team or her own ship again, she had to take action.

She and SUMI were playing hide-and-seek.

For SUMI, hide-and-seek was nothing more than a game.

For Piper, it was deadly serious.

She leaned out over the edge of her air chair and whispered, "I'm here!" Down below, she saw SUMI's head tilt upward, and she heard the creak and bump of the little robot's springy legs.

"Where, where, where?" called SUMI. When she was excited, her voice was like a stream of hiccups.

Piper swooped down behind a cabinet full of weight-lifting equipment. "Here," she whispered again.

SUMI changed direction, moving in short jumps and grunting. Piper stayed still and watched.

SUMI rounded the corner. "Ha-ha-ha-ha!" she cried, hiccuping like mad. "Found you!"

Piper smiled and shook her head as if she were disappointed. "You win this time." *But not next time,* she thought. Out loud she said, "Another game! You found me too fast. I'll hide again."

SUMI nodded her oversized head—Piper thought she looked a little like a football held up by a frame of K'nex. "Just one more time," SUMI said. "Then quantum theory lesson 71." She shut down her sight screen and began to count. "One, two, three, four . . ."

Piper took off, heading for a high metal cabinet behind the stationary bikes. Her air chair hummed so softly that she was sure SUMI couldn't hear it while she was counting. With some careful ma-neuvering, she got behind the cabinet and hovered there. *Good air chair,* she thought, and gave it a silent pat with her finger. It was like a pair of legs to her (her own didn't work at all) and, even better, like a pair of wings.

Piper had already explored every inch of the training room, looking for a way out. Every pipe, every vent, every drain, every seam or crack or dent in the wall—she'd probed each one, and at first, she'd been sure she'd find a way because the *Light Blade* wasn't very well constructed. Piper was surprised at that. She had thought it would be just like her own ship, the *Cloud Leopard,* but it was more like a rough copy, as if it had been banged together in a hurry. Still, there was nothing she could pry apart or pound on to make an opening.

The main door was the only possibility. It was equipped with a complex lock that only SUMI could release. At mealtimes, SUMI would enter the lock's code and open the door, and Niko would be there with a tray of food. Piper had thought of trying to fly out over SUMI's head, but the problem was Niko. There wasn't room for her hovercraft between his head and the top of the door.

"One hundred!" shouted SUMI. "Here I come!"

Bounce-bounce-bounce.

Piper waited until SUMI was near enough and then said, "I see you," in a loud whisper.

SUMI's head jerked upward, and she let out a stream of little hiccups. "Where? Where?"

"Right here," whispered Piper, then silently flew upward and banked left. "Here," she whispered again.

SUMI spun around, and her springy legs contracted. She bounded toward Piper's voice. "Can't *find* you!" she cried. When she was distressed, her stern machine voice became a squeak, like a rusted joint.

Piper zoomed to the upper level of the training room, looping behind SUMI. "I'm here!" she called, and at the same time, she pulled out the spoon she'd pinched from her breakfast and dropped it. It clattered to the floor, clanging off the pull-up bars on the way down.

"Gotcha now!" squeaked SUMI. She bounced like a small, top-heavy rabbit toward the sound as Piper swept down toward the locked door and hovered just above it. She tilted her air chair a bit and knocked on the door: rap-rappa-rap-rap—the way

Niko knocked when he came with the food tray. Then she did a fast vertical lift, halted far up toward the ceiling, and watched as SUMI turned and came toward the door in quick leaps.

It's going to work, Piper thought. *Just five seconds more, and that door will be open, and I'll swoop down and fly through.* She'd be free, then— at least, free in the *Light Blade*. Once she was free, she would . . . well, she wasn't sure what. But somehow she would get back to the *Cloud Leopard*.

She'd left her home ship on what she thought was an errand of mercy. The call had come through the intership communication line: Anna, the Omega team leader, was badly hurt. She needed help. Would Piper please come?

She'd gone, and instantly they'd grabbed her and locked her up.

Luckily, the *Light Blade* training room was immense—as big as her elementary school gym. There were a hundred places to hide in this cluttered room, especially for someone who could fly. Piper, of course, was an expert flier—and now she was about to escape.

SUMI reached up for the door handle.

Piper leaned forward, ready.

At that moment, someone knocked on the door from the *outside*: rap-rappa-rap-rap.

"Heard you the first time!" SUMI said. She pulled the door open, and Piper's heart sank like a stone. There stood Niko with the lunch tray. No way Piper could fly over his head.

She forced a cheerful look onto her face. "Hi, Niko," she said, swooping down to the floor. "Hey, you're looking better." When he returned from Infinity, he'd been near death from after collecting Stinger spores, and she'd had to use all her medical training to save him.

"I *am* better," Niko said. "Looks like I'm going to live. Thanks to you." He smiled.

"I'm really glad," said Piper. She felt a moment of hope. Niko was grateful. Maybe he'd help her! But the next moment, Anna and Siena came up behind him, and though Niko shot her a look of sympathy, he said nothing. The three of them blocked the door like a wall.

Piper almost lost it. She had to clap a hand over her mouth to keep from crying out in despair. How was she *ever* going to get out of this room? She didn't approve of the word *hopeless*. But right then it was almost the way she felt.

Still, she managed a grin. "Hi, everyone," she said. "Are we having a meeting?"

"*We* are," said Anna coldly. "Not you."

Niko set the lunch tray on a counter. "The ZRKs tried something new today," he said. "It's—"

Anna interrupted him. "Let's go," she said briskly. She turned and left the room, and the others followed her. Siena sent her a backward glance. What did it mean? Piper couldn't tell.

7

2

On the *Cloud Leopard's* navigation deck, the Alpha team gathered to hear from Chris about their next destination.

Dash Conroy leaned against a console, staring out the wraparound window at the view of the star streaks that crossed the sky when the ship was in Gamma Speed. He was feeling a little tired but wasn't going to show it. As the Alpha team leader, he couldn't afford to be tired. Next to him was Chris, the crew member who looked like a normal teenager but was actually an alien with some kind of super-brain. Chris was cool, but always a little stiff and formal.

"Tomorrow," Chris said in his usual official tone, "we will be landing on the planet Tundra. It's covered with ice and snow and is extremely cold. As far as we know, it has only two life-forms: ice crawlers and snow locusts. The ice crawlers are our target. The element we need, which is called zero crystals, is the coldest known substance in the universe and comes from inside an ice crawler."

"If Tundra is covered with ice, what do ice crawlers eat?" Carly Diamond, the team's second-in-command, wanted to know. Getting the facts straight—that was her specialty.

"They eat the snow locusts," Chris said. "When the locusts swarm, the ice crawler creeps inside the swarm and then curls itself up like a pill bug and rolls down a slope, becoming a ball of snow and insects. Then it eats its way out."

"Kind of a boring diet," said Gabriel Parker, expert navigator and wisecracker. "Bugs washed down with snow water."

"Boring but complete," said Chris. "An ice crawler gets both protein and liquid that way. After it's eaten, it falls into a deep sleep. That's your moment. That's when you go for the zero crystals."

"How do we get the crystals out of the creature?" Dash asked.

"You'll have a special extraction instrument," said Chris. "I call it the Talon—you'll know why when you see it. It pierces the skin and draws out the zero crystals. The crystals flow through the crawler's body the way blood flows through ours. They run through a system of capillaries just below an ice crawler's skin. They're what create a balance between the crawler and the temperature outside so the crawler can survive in Tundra's climate."

"So we stab the ice crawler?" Dash asked. "Do we need to kill it?"

"No, no," Chris answered. "Not necessary at all. In any case, we don't have the tools to kill it. It's a massive creature. You won't have to go deep to find the crystals. What you want to do is to scratch the skin just deeply enough to reach them. It's a delicate task, not a violent one."

Carly made a face. "Does an ice crawler mind being scratched?"

"It's hard to tell," said Chris. "We're not sure how much of a nervous system an ice crawler has. It is a very primitive animal."

"Like a dinosaur?" said Gabriel hopefully. "We're good at dinosaurs."

"No, not at all like that. Not nearly as fast-moving."

Good, thought Dash. A big, slow animal should be easy to deal with.

"Your first step will be to locate your weapon, the Talon," Chris said. "I stashed two of them on my original voyage, just in case. Once you've retrieved the Talon, you'll go in search of an ice crawler. I'll give you coordinates for a likely location. If you're quick and careful, all should go smoothly."

Dash thought it didn't sound so bad. The planet would be freezing cold, but no Raptogons, no warlords fighting over molten metal, no pirates, no Stingers—that sounded pretty good. They'd get this one done fast, and there would be only one more to go. Maybe they'd even make up some of the time they'd lost on the Aqua Gen planet so he wouldn't have to worry about running out of his antiaging serum. *This* mission should be no problem. He was going to be just fine.

"One last thing," said Chris. "Don't underestimate the cold on Tundra. One second of exposure is all it takes to freeze your skin."

Was Chris reading his mind? Dash thought that sounded like a warning meant just for him.

After Chris's briefing, Gabe left the navigation deck feeling a little disappointed that he wasn't on the extraction team this time; Tundra sounded cool—*really* cool. He'd be waving good-bye as Dash and Carly got into the transport ship, and after that, he'd be pretty much alone on the *Cloud Leopard*. There'd be Chris, but he had been disappearing a lot recently. He kept saying he had something important to check on, but he never said what the important thing was.

And really, that was perfect. Without Chris, it would be easier to put his top-secret plan into action. The *Cloud Leopard* would be exiting Gamma Speed soon, and Gabriel would be the one to guide the ship in its descent into orbit around Tundra. So step one of his plan would have to happen right now.

He ducked into a portal to the tubes, and after a few fast curves and swoops, he popped out in the training room. "STEAM!" he called. "Where are you?"

The little training robot came out from behind a simulation machine and shuffled toward Gabriel, swiveling his head. "Yes sir," said STEAM, "coming, yes sir!"

"I have to check something," Gabriel said. "I'm

going to put you on standby for a minute." Gabriel went to the computer screen at the side of the room, which held the program that was STEAM's "brain." Quickly, Gabriel brought up some code on the display and tweaked a few lines of it. "Remote access request," he muttered to himself. "Cut line three hundred twenty-nine Z, reconnect alternative route eleven-fourteen, clear the under channel . . ." His fingers darted over the touch screen. He sat back. "That should help," he said. "Okay, STEAM, bringing you up again."

STEAM's blue eyes flashed, and he made a sort of humming sound. "Yes sir," he said.

Gabriel grinned at him and patted his metal robot head. "At ease, soldier!" Gabriel said, and then strolled out of the training room as if he'd just been in there doing a few pull-ups.

It was time to exit Gamma Speed. Gabriel headed for the nearest portal. It was true, he thought: he was brilliant. He sent a mental message to Piper: Help is on the way!

The Alpha team took their seats on the navigation deck and checked their seat belts. Gabriel put on his flight glasses in case manual control became necessary.

"Ready?" said Dash.

"Ready," said the rest of the crew, all together.

"Exiting Gamma Speed." Dash said it calmly. Gabe had brought the *Cloud Leopard* down into a planetary orbit three times before by now. Strange to think that such an extraordinary thing could become almost routine.

But routine or not, it was always a rough few minutes, as if a gigantic fist had grabbed the ship and was shaking it like a toy. Everyone's teeth rattled. Their bodies were pressed backward, hard, by g-forces. Stomachs churned, hands gripped chair arms, bones jumped and jolted—and then they were through. The ship's normal gravity setting returned. The roar of the engines ceased, and they were in smooth and quiet orbit around the planet Tundra.

"That's a *planet*?" said Gabriel, staring out the great front window. "It looks like a scoop of vanilla ice cream."

"It does." Dash had to agree. "Only not as inviting as ice cream."

"All right already," said Carly, who wasn't much for fantasy. "It's ice. Every square inch of that planet is below the freezing point—way, way below."

"I feel sorry for the creatures that live there," said Gabriel. "I hope they have fireplaces or hot tubs where they can go to warm up."

Carly rolled her eyes. "Whatever lives there would *hate* heat. They're adapted to live in the cold."

Of course, thought Dash. Heat would be an enemy for the creatures of Tundra, just as for him, a boy who'd grown up in Florida, cold was an enemy.

STEAM rolled in and beeped. "Ice, ice, baby!" he said, and the Alpha team laughed.

Dash unclicked his seat belt, and the others followed. "Time to go bundle up."

3

The *Light Blade* had exited Gamma Speed, and like the Alpha team, the Omega team gazed in awe at the strange white planet.

For Anna, the first order of business was to check in with Earth. She turned to Colin, who sat at the controls. "Get us the connection," she said.

Colin gave a curt nod. He flicked some switches and turned some dials. He spoke into the transmitter, and his voice crossed light-years between the ship and Earth: "*Light Blade* here," he said. "Come in, Commander Ike Phillips."

A thin squeal was the response.

Colin frowned and shoved his glasses farther up on his nose. He gave a dial another twist. "Come in, Sir," he said again, and this time a distant voice answered—surprisingly clear.

"Phillips here. What's the report?"

"I'll take over," said Anna. She took Colin's place at the transmitter. Briskly, she told Ike about the Infinity mission—where they'd ridden winged horses through underground tunnels and battled giant eels to bring back an element called Stinger spores. She paused briefly in case Ike wanted to say *Great job* or something like it. Ike was the genius behind their voyage, the visionary who'd known that she and her team were the ones who should fly these missions. Even if he wasn't always easy to like, Anna wanted to make him proud.

But Ike didn't offer a comment. "What else?" he said.

"We have a prisoner," Anna said. She told him about Piper. "With her on board, the Alphas aren't likely to try any nasty tricks. Plus now we have two medics, just in case."

"Not bad," said Ike. "So listen, crew. You're closer to the end, just two elements left to get. I want everyone in top form. No mistakes. We're talking about . . ."

His voice faded.

"We're losing you, sir," Anna called.

Colin reached over her shoulder and adjusted a switch.

". . . future of the planet," came Ike's voice again, overly loud all of a sudden. "When you get back—"

The signal weakened again, and Ike's voice faded to a distant whisper.

"Got it, Commander," said Anna. "Signing off."

Soon, she thought, when they returned to Earth with the elements needed to fuel the planet into the far future, Ike Phillips would give them the praise they had earned. From then on, the management of Earth's power would be in his capable hands, not in the hands of his dim-witted son, Shawn, or the government Shawn stood for. And the glory (Anna had to admit she liked glory) would be all for the Omega team.

It was time for the Tundra briefing. Anna surveyed her team, gathered on the navigation deck. They were battle-hardened by now. They had conquered four planets; they had raced against the Alpha team and—sometimes—outmaneuvered them. Their long journey would soon be drawing to a close, and Anna wanted it to end the right way: with their victory.

Whatever it would take to accomplish that goal, that's what Anna was willing to do. If it meant giving

orders now and then that her team didn't like—
well, that came with being a leader. She gazed at
the faces before her and thought, *They've done it so
far. They can do it again.*

"Everyone *listen*," she said. She glared at
Niko Rodriguez and Siena Moretti, her second-in-
command. They had been whispering, but Niko
went quiet immediately. He knew not to mess with
Anna when she was in command mode. And yet
Niko had urgent things to say to Siena, things that
Anna couldn't know. He nodded to her very slightly
so that no one else would notice. Siena knew what
the nod meant: *Later.*

Anna assumed her gravest expression. The best
way to keep her crew safe, she knew, was to make
sure they understood from the start how dangerous
the task ahead of them was.

"Tomorrow," she said, "we will be landing on
the planet Tundra. It's a place so cold that exposed
skin will freeze instantaneously—that is, it will get
numb, turn blue, and die." She paused to let the
seriousness of this sink in. They all had to *think*
about what this would mean.

Each person was thinking something different.

Ravi was thinking about snow. Since his home was in Mumbai, India, he'd never seen snow. He looked forward to it. There might be time to have a snowball fight. Maybe even make a snowman.

Niko, the team's medic, was thinking, *Incorrect. Frozen flesh does not turn blue; it turns white.*

Siena was thinking, *Anna would be more impressive if she didn't try so hard to be impressive.*

SUMI, who had left Piper securely locked into the training room, was simply entering all the information she heard into her thousand-terabyte database.

And then there was Colin, who was different from the others on the team. He knew a lot more than they did about the history of this voyage and about the planets the Voyagers would visit. He was also a clone—not a human clone, but an alien clone, a duplicate of the real alien, Chris. He watched Anna intently as she spoke. Whatever he was thinking, it didn't show on his face. There was nothing in his eyes but cold determination.

Anna went on. "Ice crawlers are extremely large," she said, "and there aren't all that many of them; snow locusts are tiny, only about an inch long, and there are hundreds of millions of them."

"Do they sting?" asked Niko, who had recent and unpleasant memories about being stung.

"I don't think so," Anna said with a quick glance at Colin. He nodded, and she said, "No, they don't sting. It's the ice crawlers that are likely to be dangerous. They are huge."

"How huge?" asked Siena. *Huge* was such a vague word. Siena liked information to be detailed and specific.

"As big as a . . ." Anna hesitated, and Siena could tell she didn't know and was about to make something up. "About as big as a car," she said, and quickly changed the subject. "The point is," she continued, "that ice crawlers are our target. We need zero crystals, and they're inside the ice crawlers."

"Inside?" Niko was puzzled. "How do we—"

"You'll get that information later," Anna interrupted. "Colin will brief the extraction team." She switched on a screen behind her. "Here's how the team will get around on Tundra."

The screen showed a picture of a sleek, high-powered snowmobile. It was silver, with red blades. "It's called the Cheetah, because it can get up to seventy-five miles an hour."

There was a sigh of admiration from Niko.

"But you won't be going, Niko," Anna said. "You're just back from a mission that almost killed you. You need to get up some strength before you're going anywhere. The Tundra team will be Ravi and me."

Niko's heart sank, but he didn't show it. It was true that he still wasn't himself after what had happened on Infinity. He gave a quick nod.

Ravi, on the other hand, was thrilled.

Siena tried to catch Niko's eye and gave a small shrug. They hated it when Anna was right.

4

Early the next morning, Dash sat alone at the controls of the *Cloud Leopard*, speaking urgently. He had contacted the team's commander back on Earth. "They *kidnapped* Piper," he said. "They knew she'd go and help if Anna was in danger. It was all a trick."

There was a moment of silence, and then Shawn's voice came through, clear and somber. "That's terrible news," he said. "But I don't see what you can do about it at this point. Your Tundra mission has to take priority. At least Piper will be safe on the *Light Blade*. The Omega team wouldn't do anything to harm her."

"I guess not," said Dash, though he wasn't sure.

"How's your health?" Shawn asked.

"I'm all right," Dash said. He wasn't sure about this either. There were times when his strength suddenly failed. It always came back, though. He was probably fine.

"And you leave for Tundra in about an hour?"

"Fifty-five minutes," said Dash.

"Good fortune to you," Shawn said. "You'll need it."

And although Dash had all the information about this next planet and knew everything was ready for the mission, he felt a shiver go through him.

He shook it off. "Thanks." This might be a good time to squeeze in a little fun and give his worries a rest. He left the navigation deck and headed down the central corridor toward the relaxation room.

No one was there, just as he'd hoped. Someone had left half a bagel on the counter, and a couple of pillows had been tossed on the floor. How come the ZRKs hadn't cleaned this up? Dash made a mental note to do it himself—or to ask a ZRK Commander to handle it. But he didn't have time now. He went to the portal on the far side of the room. On the touch screen beside it, he marked the points of the route he'd planned through the maze of transport tubes that ran within the core of the ship.

It was a contest between the members of the Alpha team—a sport they'd invented for themselves. Part of it—zooming through the twists and loops and dips of the tubes—was pure pleasure. Another part was a puzzle: Who could find the longest route between two points of the maze? Dash had memorized the map that was posted next to every port, and he studied it when he wasn't dealing with the duties of being team captain. He'd draw different connections between ports, try them out, keeping track of his time; then he'd draw again and try again, always looking for a new longer route.

But he kept making wrong turns. He'd make a U when he shouldn't have and end up in the dining room, or he'd go sharply upward and find himself in the boys' dorm. Each time, he'd store the error in his mental map; he never made the same mistake twice. He would find the route, he knew. If he was lucky, he'd find it today.

He reached up, took hold of the overhead bar, and swung himself inside. Instantly, the rushing current of air caught him and swept him forward, first steeply upward, and then plummeting downward. His imagination flashed pictures before his eyes. He was a salmon speeding upstream, he was an eagle plunging toward its prey, he was a fast car on a freeway swerving left, then right—his mind worked as hard as his muscles, marking the turns, mapping the tangle of tubes.

Carly Diamond whizzed by him at an intersection, her long black hair streaking out behind her. "Dash, where are you going?" she called back. "We're leaving in less than an hour!"

He didn't answer. Already he could feel it: pulling air down into his lungs was harder, and his heart was pounding faster. He'd be all right, though. He wasn't *that* tired. He kept going.

He ignored the hammering of his heart. He took the S-curve that led upward—and saw, just as he passed, the turn that would have led to the path he had meant to take.

Instead, the maze spit him out into the rec room, where he crumpled to his knees, coughing so hard he thought his ribs might break. His heart was racing—a pulse of a hundred and ten, his Mobile Tech Band told him, way too fast. His oxygen level was low too.

Luckily, the rec room was empty. He couldn't be seen like this. No one but Chris and Piper knew

he was too old for this journey, and that he could survive it only with the help of daily injections to slow down his metabolism. But they might guess if they saw him weak and sick. He took some deep breaths. He focused his mind on the thudding of his heart and slowed it down. He checked his MTB again, which told him he was doing better and also that forty-eight minutes were left before the exploration team was scheduled to leave for Tundra. He had time. He'd go once more.

He got to his feet. On the touch screen beside the portal, he entered the corrected route. He swung himself in and sped along until he came to the turn he'd meant to take before. Woo-hoo! This time he did it right. Curve after curve followed, downward slopes and upward climbs, and at last he tumbled out onto a hard, shiny white floor. He checked his time. He'd done it—the longest route yet. He pumped a fist in the air. And then he looked around and realized he had no idea where he was. No other room in the entire ship looked like this.

5

Dash got to his feet in the unfamiliar corridor and looked around. He was breathing hard, but now he was more excited than tired. Slowly, he walked to the right, examining the wall as he went. His fingers felt it before he saw it: the almost invisible outline of a door in the wall. Where a doorknob should be, there was an oval indentation with a strip of metal across it. Dash took hold of the strip and pulled, and the door swung open easily.

Inside was a single room, wide and high-ceilinged and full of light, and in the center of the room stood something that looked at first like a battered old blimp. Dash stepped forward.

"Finally," said a voice, making Dash jump.

A hatch in the blimp-shaped thing rose with a

creak, and Dash realized he was looking at a rocket ship, ancient and strange, but clearly meant for space travel. It was like a small oddly shaped version of the *Cloud Leopard*—as if the *Cloud Leopard* had somehow swallowed another ship and was carrying it in its belly.

Suddenly, Dash couldn't catch his breath. His head was spinning, and darkness was crowding in around the edges of his vision. He felt his knees giving way, and then he was on the floor.

The same voice spoke. "You're in bad shape." His arm was lifted. "Let me check your vitals." There was a pause. Dash was sinking into a foggy darkness. The voice came again, as if from a distance. "All right, don't move. You need a shot right now."

Some fast footsteps. Some clicking sounds. Then a prick in the arm, and slowly, Dash's vision cleared and some strength returned. He looked up to find Chris's face, familiar and kind. He tried to say *thank you,* but the words came out blurred. Even so, Chris understood. "You're welcome," he said, smiling.

But the smile faded quickly. "This was a bad one," he said. "All your signs were drastically low.

You just can't keep up this pace. You have to slow down if you're going to last the trip."

"I can't slow down," Dash said, his voice a little stronger now. "I'm the leader."

"You won't be any good to the team if you're dead," said Chris. "I mean it."

"But I need to go on this mission. How can I lead if I'm not even on the planet?"

Chris looked like he was going to argue, but Dash jumped in again.

"With Piper gone, we're down a team member," Dash reminded him.

"Well, if you won't sit this one out, at least be careful," Chris said. He stood and reached for Dash. "Can you get up?"

Dash struggled to his feet, using Chris's arm to steady himself.

"Where am I?"

"You're in a carefully hidden space directly under the engine room, accessible only via the tubes."

Dash stood. The blackness swam up before his eyes, and he staggered but stayed upright and again his vision cleared. "I'm fine," he said.

Chris gave him a doubting look but said nothing,

just motioned him up two steps and inside the smaller ship.

Dash looked around in wonder. They were in a control room. An array of lights blinked red, green, and yellow, and something rumbled, making the walls and floor shudder. "What *is* this thing?" said Dash. "What's it doing here?"

"It's an old friend of mine," said Chris. "This is the ship that carried me on my journey to Earth."

His journey to Earth. Dash almost forgot sometimes that Chris was *not* from Earth. He looked like a human being, and—usually—he acted like one too.

Dash was confused. "You came to Earth in *this*?" With Chris at his side, he walked around it and peered in the open hatch. What he saw amazed him. Once, he could tell, this had been a sleek, compact ship. Its hull was still a lustrous silver in places, and there was a line of graceful loops and slashes on the side that must be writing, but not in any script Dash had ever seen. He peered in an oval window at the rear and saw a tiny, perfect cabin, with a narrow bed and panels in the walls that must open into cabinets. Across one end of the room lay a person-sized cylinder of clear glass.

Dash pointed at it. "What was that for?"

"I made parts of the trip in there," said Chris. "Suspended animation."

"For months at a time?" Dash asked.

"Years at a time."

On the far side of the ship was another small window. Through it, Dash saw what looked like a lab, with coils and flasks and instruments. Up against the ship's wall, he saw a glass case, and inside the case a rack holding twelve test tubes, each one filled with a crystal-clear liquid.

"What's in the tubes?" he asked.

"It's the DNA we collected back at camp, from everyone."

"What's it doing *here*?"

"I thought it might be useful."

Dash raised his eyebrows. "Really? For what?"

"It doesn't matter," Chris replied. "I was wrong." He pressed his lips together, staring down at the tubes as if they were living things that had died.

Dash wasn't sure he wanted to let that one go. They'd had so many secrets on the ship. . . . Was this another one? Did Piper know about these DNA samples? Unfortunately, it wasn't like he could ask her now. And that was an even bigger problem.

Before he knew it, Chris was guiding him back toward the front of his ship, and his curiosity about the much larger secret—this hidden vehicle—took over.

Dash peered in at the command center. Parts of the console were hanging open, revealing tangles of wires and circuit boards and tiny flickering lights. A couple of large red lights—clearly warning lights—flashed steadily off and on. On the floor was a box full of jumbled equipment. Dash recognized pliers and a screwdriver; the rest was mysterious.

"Looks like it's in bad shape," Dash said.

"It is," said Chris.

"So why have you kept it?" Dash asked. "Is this sort of a museum, this room?"

"Not at all," said Chris. He motioned to the other side of the ship and pointed to a bundle of heavy cables that led into the far wall. "I'm going to tell you something no one else knows," he said. "I want you to keep it to yourself."

"Okay," Dash said. He was a little troubled about keeping another secret from his team.

"This ship is the brain of the *Cloud Leopard*. The system we're running—the one that manages everything from night-lights to interstellar navigation—is the system built into this old clunker. It guided me on the trip from my home planet to Earth, and now it's guiding us on the return. Without this ship, we'd be no better than a chunk of rock, lost in space."

Dash wondered if his mind was still a little foggy. This broken-down wreck was the brain of the *Cloud Leopard*?

He turned back to Chris. "You're kidding me, right?"

"Unfortunately, no. Everything I've told you is true, but there's something else: as you can see, this ship is not exactly in top shape. Remember when the kitchen lights went out that time? And remember when we got off course between Meta Prime and Aqua Gen? Those were system glitches, the first one trivial and the second potentially fatal. You know why I so often disappear? Because I have to work on this thing all the time, adjusting and patching and recoding, trying to keep it working long enough to get us there and back."

Dash was speechless. His mind whirled. He had a sudden vision of the *Cloud Leopard* as a rock— no, a tiny pebble—in the vastness of space, drifting through the dark, its brain having blinked out. There was terror in that vision, but he shunted it away. "Will we make it?" he managed to say.

"I'm doing my best," said Chris, which didn't really answer the question, but Dash didn't mind. He might not *want* to hear the answer.

Chris gave Dash a long, serious look. "Now you know: we both have a secret. We both have to do everything we can to make it to the end of this journey. Promise me you'll take care of yourself."

"I will," said Dash. He rapped lightly on the side of the ship. "And you promise to take care of this rotting heap of junk."

Down in the *Cloud Leopard*'s docking bay, the ZRKs were busy with last-minute touch-ups to the transport ship, the *Cloud Cat*. They buzzed around it in swarms. The cockpit was full of them, hovering over the control panel, testing lights and poking buttons and wiping down the seats. There were ZRKs checking fuel gauges, ZRKs polishing the windshield, ZRKs oiling the landing gear and adjusting the thruster angles and dusting off the roof. The air was loud with their chattering, whizzing sounds.

A few minutes before launch time, Chris, Dash, and Carly arrived in the engine room.

"All right," said Chris. "Let's get this show on the road." He turned to the equipment cabinet beside the docking bay door. From it he took out the special body suits Dash and Carly would wear to protect themselves against the extreme cold. They were dark red, to show up against the white of Tundra, and they had helmets that looked like the ones a deep-sea diver would wear. On the back was a pack for tools and supplies, and each suit also held a small oxygen tank with a filter that heated the air they would breathe. "You can't breathe the air of Tundra," Chris said. "Don't even try. It will freeze your lungs." He clapped his hands a couple of times, loudly. "ZRKs finished?" he called.

Apparently they were. They all flew off.

"Okay," said Chris. "Let's load up."

Dash opened the hatch at the back of the *Cloud Cat*. Together, he and Carly hoisted in TULIP. Dash had had some doubts about taking her. She carried the element from Meta Prime inside her, and it seemed like a huge risk to bring an element with them. But Chris had insisted. "She's fearless because she feels no pain," he said. "She can go places you can't." Carly was glad the little robot was coming, so Dash didn't object.

They got her settled in the cargo space, next to the Streak, the speedy little snowmobile they'd use to get around on Tundra's surface.

"When we get back," Dash said, "we're rescuing Piper, right? Whatever it takes."

"Right," said Chris.

"Even if we have to trick them," said Carly. "The way they tricked us."

"Right again," said Chris.

"Even if we have to storm the *Light Blade!*" cried Gabriel. "With our laser swords and zap guns!" He slashed an imaginary weapon through the air and made zapping noises.

"I hope zap guns won't be necessary," Chris said, laughing a little. "Especially since we don't have any. Let's go."

Gabriel smiled to himself. It was all just for show; he had other ideas that he wasn't ready to talk about.

Dash and Carly got into their protective suits. It took a lot of zipping and buckling and clamping. When they were done, they both looked about twice their usual size.

"You won't be able to hear each other in these," said Chris. "So there's a two-way radio built in." He showed them how to turn it on.

"Alpha One calling Alpha Two," said Dash. "Come in, Alpha Two."

"Hearing you loud and clear, Alpha One," said Carly.

They grinned at each other through the thick clear plastic of their helmets.

"You should be able to communicate with the Omega team too," Chris said. "Once you encounter them—as I'm sure you will—just flip this switch to change frequencies."

Chris opened the *Cloud Cat*'s door and got into the pilot's seat. He would fly the *Cloud Cat* down onto Tundra's surface, leave Dash and Carly, and return to the ship. Dash and Carly settled into the two seats in back of him. Before Dash flicked the switch that would close the hatch, he turned to wave at Gabriel. "Take care of things back here!"

"No problem!" Gabriel called. "See you soon!"

I hope so, thought Dash.

"Ready for launch," Chris said. He touched a screen, and the thrusters fired.

On the *Light Blade*, Siena was reading in the library. She paused with her finger on the screen to listen when she heard Anna's voice through the intercom system.

"Ready for launch to Tundra," Anna called out. "Ravi and Colin, meet me in the docking bay. Siena and Niko, to the navigation deck. Make it quick!"

Nine minutes later, Niko and Siena watched as the *Clipper* swooped down toward Tundra. When it was gone, Niko turned to Siena and said, "Okay, then. Back to work."

"Right," said Siena.

But neither one of them moved.

Niko gave Siena a sideways glance. "I've been thinking about Piper," he said.

"I have too," Siena admitted.

"I don't feel good about seeing her locked up."

"Neither do I," Siena said.

"Without her, I'd probably be dead. I couldn't have cured my own sting after Infinity," Niko said.

Siena nodded. "I feel worse and worse. And not just about Piper. It's Colin and Anna and their . . . leadership. I think we have to do something."

"Yes," said Niko. "We need a plan."

As the *Cloud Cat* sailed through the dense Tundra atmosphere, Dash closed his eyes and breathed deeply and steadily, calming his heart and filling his mind with pictures of power: a soaring bird, its black wings twenty feet wide; a crouching cougar, every muscle ready. He wanted to push aside the uneasy feelings he had about this planet of ice and snow.

Carly obviously didn't feel the same. She leaned against the window, looking out with a hungry stare, as if she couldn't wait to get to Tundra and tackle an ice crawler. That wasn't quite it, Dash knew; what Carly was eager for was driving the Streak. She'd reached the top skill level on the simulator ages ago and was more than ready for the real thing.

Behind them, TULIP made small chuckling noises, her way of expressing excitement.

It took only a short time to shoot through Tundra's atmosphere and come within sight of its surface.

"Nearly there," said Chris. "You're clear on the coordinates for the cave, right?"

They both lifted their left hands and checked their MTBs. They'd entered the numbers that would lead them to the cave where, long ago, Chris had hidden what he called the Talons.

"Yep, got the numbers," said Dash.

"And the numbers for ice crawlers?"

"Got them." Dash and Carly said it at exactly

the same time, which made them turn and smile at each other. Once again: a team on a mission. Dash began to feel better.

Chris fired the landing jets, and the transport ship slowed and descended. Forgetting his worries, Dash stared out the window at the terrible beauty of this planet. Snow white and ice blue as far as his eyes could see, and all its shapes jagged, pointed, and fierce-looking as wolf teeth. They came down toward the edge of a vast plain and landed, spraying snow in great plumes to either side, just where the flat snow-covered ground began to slant upward, where the foothills of a range of peaks began.

Chris flicked the switch that opened the ship's back hatch and lowered the ramp for the snowmobile.

"Ready for some fresh air?" Dash radioed to Carly.

"Bring it on," she radioed back.

They gave the thumbs-up signal to Chris, and he opened the doors.

Outside, the wind hit them, icy and powerful. They leaned against it and made their way to the back of the transport ship. Carly climbed the ramp and brought TULIP outside, and then she and Dash took hold of the Streak and slid it down onto the ground. They opened its doors, hoisted in TULIP, and got in themselves.

Carly tapped here and there on the controls, and the engine growled and roared into life. She and Dash strapped themselves securely into their seats and then Carly gripped the steering lever and smiled. Because of all her exercises on the simulator, this machine felt utterly familiar. She had no fears about driving it. But when she raised her eyes and looked through the windscreen, she understood that no simulator could have prepared her for this place. It was vast beyond imagining, and not a single thing in its blazing white landscape looked remotely friendly. It *definitely* did not remind her of ice cream.

Chris's voice came to them one last time through their earpieces. "Off you go," he said. "Remember: be careful, and be quick."

Carly pressed lightly on the accelerator, and they glided out onto the surface of Tundra. When she'd driven clear of the *Cloud Cat,* she stopped, and she and Dash watched as Chris saluted them. Then the transport's thrusters fired, melting a wide track of snow, and the ship rose into the air, heading back to the *Cloud Leopard.*

Three and a half miles to the northeast of where the *Cloud Cat* had landed, a herd of ice crawlers, nearly a hundred of them, huddled together by the shore of a silvery lake. The herd sensed a change. Something unfamiliar had arrived in their territory. Awareness of it swept among them like a wind, and the crawlers rumbled. Their humped, sluglike gray bodies shuddered. A few of them, as if sniffing the air, lifted their blunt front ends. On the underside were their mouths, long slits that opened and closed and were rimmed with teeth. A few crawlers at the edge of the herd inched forward. Others followed, slowly, in a long disorderly group. What was the new thing that had come? Was it good to eat?

7

Carly and Dash sat still for a moment, gazing out at the Tundra landscape. Wind whistled around them and blew spirals of snow into the air. Carly spoke into her transmitter, and Dash heard her voice as if she were speaking right next to his ear. "First on the agenda," she said. "The cave."

"Right," said Dash. He checked his MTB and read out the coordinates that Chris had provided.

Carly pressed a button, and the motor roared. The Streak leaned and turned. Dash could see nothing but white, white, and more white as they sped along, until suddenly a strip of black rock would rear up and be gone, or they'd pass a snowdrift shaped by the wind into peaks with blue shadows. Ridges of jagged ice, cliffs that seemed to rise out of nowhere—it was a rugged landscape, where fast travel was perilous.

And yet Carly kept the racer moving at incredible speed. "I love this!" she cried. She ran the Streak up a slope and over the top, and for a few seconds, they were airborne. "Wheee!"

When they'd been speeding along for five or six minutes, Dash noticed that they were picking up a heat signal. "Slow down for a minute," he said. "Something's out there."

Carly braked. "What is it?"

"I don't know. Look at this reading." He held out his wrist.

"Maybe an ice crawler?"

"I don't think so. This thing is moving faster than any animal would."

Carly changed course, and they headed toward the signal. It wasn't long before they saw a dark dot speeding across the landscape. It could be only one thing.

"The *Light Blade* team," Dash said. "They got here before us."

Carly's voice sounded grim in Dash's ear. "All right," she said, "they're here, but they haven't found the cave. They're in the wrong place. We'll get there before them."

She stepped on the accelerator. The engine roared and screamed as Carly swung around a sharp curve.

Dash's heart was racing—full of adrenaline. *This is awesome,* he thought, but the next moment, when he glanced down at the map, a shock ran through him. "Carly, look out! Straight ahead—a crevasse! Slow down!"

Carly veered sharp right. The brakes squealed, and the racer stopped in a cloud of snow. They turned to look at each other, wide-eyed. Carly moved the Streak forward an inch at a time, until they were right at the edge of the great crack in the ice—sheer walls of deep blue plunged to an invisible bottom.

They were silent for a moment.

"We can do it easily," Carly said.

"You're sure?"

"Sure. I've jumped wider ones a hundred times on the simulator. We just have to get up speed. Come on."

She turned the Streak and drove it back the way they'd come for half a mile, then turned again in the direction of the crevasse. Dash watched the speedometer—sixty miles per hour, sixty-five, seventy—and then looked through the windshield to see the lip of the yawning crack straight ahead, and suddenly, there was air beneath them, deep blue fathoms of it. But before he knew it, the white ground was below them again, the landing so smooth and soft he hardly felt it.

Carly grinned and kept going. Dash gave her a quick, happy punch in the arm.

For a while, they sped across the snow easily, like expert skiers, riding the curves, catching air on the high dunes, never slackening their speed. Dash sat back; his tension drained away.

They crested a hill, and Dash looked out toward the horizon and saw pale, cloudlike columns rising against the sky, dipping and twirling and bending like mile-high dancers. They moved together, in an unruly crowd, maybe fifty of them, maybe more, sweeping across the snowy land toward a region of low hills.

"Uh-oh," said Carly. "Look." She pointed to the west, where a line of darkness showed above the mountains.

"A storm," said Dash. "Do you think we're headed for it?"

"I think it's headed for us," Carly answered, and immediately, Dash could see that it was. The dark line was rising, covering more and more of the sky.

"The wind's picking up," Carly said. "I can feel it trying to blow us sideways." She tightened her grip on the steering wheel.

Snow struck against the windshield, hard, like little pebbles, and the clouds came lower, and then they were inside the blizzard. Wind drove the snow at them in a blinding spiral.

"I can't see anything!" Carly wrestled with the steering wheel, trying to steady the Streak against the wind howling around them. "We have to slow down."

Dash pressed against the glass, squinting, trying to see through the swirling white. "Looks like a gap in the cliff up ahead," he said, pointing. "Can we get there?"

"I don't know!" Carly's voice had an edge of fear. "This wind! It's so strong!"

The noise was thunderous. A powerful gust struck them from the side, and Dash felt the Streak tipping him toward the ground. "We're going over!" he shouted.

Carly fought hard, but when the wind caught their underside, it pushed full force, and the snow-mobile leaned and fell, leaving them sitting side-ways, strapped into their seats, one above the other. The driver's side door was now the roof door.

Carly clicked its lock and pushed upward with all her might. The door sprang open, letting in showers of snow. "Climbing out!" Carly radioed. She undid her seat belt and gripped the edge of the door and hoisted herself through, feeling a moment of gratitude for all those pull-ups STEAM had made her do. Lying across the Streak's side, she stretched an arm down toward Dash. He grabbed her hand, she pulled, and he made his way up and out.

What struck him first was not the wind, not the driving snow, but the cold. It seemed to come right through his protective suit and find its way into his bones. He was stunned by it.

They both were.

But they had to move. They dropped down to ground level and stood beside the Streak, which lay with its runners facing them. "Grab the top runner,"

Dash said. Carly did, and he did too, and they both pulled on it with all their strength. But the Streak, though it ran across snow as lightly as a water spider, was built of heavy stuff, and they couldn't budge it. They walked around it and tried hoisting it up from the other side. "Look," said Carly, "this whole part is already frozen into the snow."

If they'd had a long board and a rock, they might have made a lever to lift the Streak, but Tundra was treeless. If they'd had a way to boil water, they might have freed the Streak by melting the ice that held it. But though they had water with them, they had no stove to heat it on. "We could make a fire," said Dash, but without hope. What fire would survive in this wind?

They heard some scraping sounds, and in the open hatch of the Streak, a trapezoidal head appeared.

"TULIP!" cried Carly. "We forgot her!"

They lifted up TULIP's heavy little body and set her down on the snow. Her belly glowed orange.

"Good call, Carly!" shouted Dash.

Carly smiled. "The cold never bothered me anyway."

TULIP was already at work. Heat beamed out from

her middle at the ice locking the Streak to the ground, and in a few minutes, the ice was water. Dash and Carly slid their fat-gloved hands underneath, found the ridge at the top of the window, and pulled with all their might. When the ship came free, they backed up to it and pushed with the force of their whole bodies. The Streak groaned, creaked, and at last sat upright on its runners.

Carly cheered. "Done!" she cried out. "Let's go!"

But Dash stood still. A wave of weakness swept over him. His body felt heavy as stone. He couldn't show Carly he was breaking down, so he leaned against a snowbank and pretended to be tinkering with his wrist tech settings. "Hold on a second," he said. "I need to make an adjustment here." His heart was pounding at his ribs—thud, thud, thud— way too fast.

"What adjustment? What's wrong?"

"Just have to get these coordinates . . ." *Breathe,* he told himself.

"Do it while we ride!" yelled Carly. "We have to hurry!"

But it was several seconds before Dash could make his legs move. By the time he got into the

Streak and fastened his straps, Carly was vibrating with impatience. "I don't understand what took so long," she said.

Dash spoke as strongly as he could, which was hard, knowing he was lying. "I had to get the settings right. It's tough to do it when we're going a thousand miles an hour."

For a second, they scowled at each other.

But there was no time for that. The next second, they were off again, moving slowly at first through the diminishing storm, and then fast as the storm passed over them and they came into the clear.

Carly resumed top speed. They followed the route through the valley, climbed toward the mountain pass, and after some wrong turns and mistaken stops, they came to the dark mouth of a cave at the top of a long, boulder-strewn slope. It would have been a moment to celebrate except for one thing: the snowmobile from the *Light Blade* was already there.

8

Gabriel stood at the console of the *Cloud Leopard*'s navigation deck, watching a dot on a screen that showed the *Cloud Cat*'s progress toward Tundra. The dot moved down and down. A yellow starburst flared. That was the landing. The *Cloud Cat* was dropping off Dash and Carly. A few minutes later, another yellow burst signaled that the *Cloud Cat* was on its way back. Good. Time to go and have a talk with Chris.

He hopped into the nearest portal and sped through the maze. In seconds, he was at the other end of the ship, tumbling out onto the floor of the engine room. He waited, and soon he heard the outer door of the docking bay opening, the transport ship powering down and rolling in, and the outer door closing. For a moment, there was quiet, and then the inner door slid upward and in came the *Cloud Cat*. Chris climbed down from the cockpit.

Gabriel bounded toward him. "Did everything go okay?"

"Yeah," said Chris. "No problems."

"Pretty cold down there?"

"You can't imagine. All okay here?"

"Fine. It's only been about half an hour since you left." Gabriel grinned. "Not a lot can go wrong in half an hour."

"Well, actually it can," said Chris. "But I'm glad it didn't."

They walked together out of the bay and up the central corridor. "I expect they'll be able to get the element in five hours or so," Chris said. "If all goes well. There's the weather to contend with, of course, and there could be some trouble dealing with the ice crawlers. But this mission ought to be a fairly quick one."

Gabriel checked the time on his MTB. "So it's eight thirty right now. That means they should be calling in at about one thirty with the signal for one of us to pick them up."

"That's right," said Chris. "And in the meantime, will you be okay on your own? A few hours of free time won't be unwelcome, I'm sure."

"I think I can suffer through them," Gabriel said.

"See you later, then. I have to go and check on—" Chris paused awkwardly. "Various matters."

"Before you go," said Gabriel, putting a hand on Chris's arm. "I have an idea. Can we talk for a second?"

"Sure. In here?" Chris led Gabriel into the rec room, and they sat down at one of the small tables. Someone had left a bagel there. "Want this?" Gabe asked, and when Chris shook his head, he picked it up and took a bite.

"So what's the idea?" Chris asked.

"We have to get Piper back," said Gabriel, chewing.

"Correct," said Chris. "Dash and I have been negotiating about it with Anna, but we haven't gotten anywhere so far."

"We have to get it done," said Gabe, "whether Anna agrees or not."

"You're right, of course. But how do we do that?"

"We go and get her," Gabriel said with a mouthful of bagel. "We take the *Cloud Cat*. We fly it right up to the *Light Blade,* and we board the ship, kind of like pirates, only *good* pirates. We find Piper, and we rescue her. Now."

"Ah," said Chris. He gave Gabriel a serious look. "But I don't see how that would work."

Gabriel put the bagel down. "Why not?"

"For one thing, how would we get the *Cloud Cat* into the *Light Blade?* I doubt that the team is just going to open up the dock doors for us."

"There must be a way."

"There will be a way," said Chris, "but I'm pretty sure that won't be it." He pushed back his chair and stood up.

"What *will* it be, then?"

"I don't know yet," said Chris. "But acting like pirates isn't it. We need a diplomatic approach." He turned and started for the door. "See you in a few hours."

Okay, thought Gabriel. His conscience was clear. He'd run his idea (most of it) by Chris, but Chris didn't like it. Chris was wrong on this one. They had a chance to rescue Piper right now, and they couldn't let this chance go by. Gabriel would just have to do it himself.

Not that he was so sorry about that.

Time was critical. He sprang up from his chair, tossed the bagel in the garbage, and headed back to the docking bay. There he climbed into the cockpit of the *Cloud Cat* and adjusted its controls to his setting. Lift. Forward power. Stabilizer. Fuel gauge. Navigation panels. *Hello, friends,* he thought.

As for the problem of getting into the *Light Blade:* Piper would take care of that. He didn't have it all lined up yet. But he would. First he had to communicate with her.

He zipped over to the training room and called to STEAM. "Come on, STEAM. We have work to do." Together, they went up the corridor to the navigation deck. The immense window showed the great curve of Tundra's surface and the black sky beyond. Not far away, standing still in space just like the *Cloud Leopard,* was the *Light Blade.* Inside it, somewhere, maybe locked in a closet or chained to a post, was Piper.

Gabriel sat down at the console and STEAM came up beside him. "We're going to do something new," Gabe said. "It's called hacking. We're going to hack into SUMI."

STEAM flashed a green light. "Something new," he said. "New is good. But why?"

"Great question," said Gabriel. "It's because we want to communicate with Piper, and that's the only way I can think of to do it. Tech-wise, you and that SUMI robot they mentioned are probably a lot the same. So it should be possible. All we have to do is get a communications channel open between us and the *Light Blade,* and from there, we can get into their network. That shouldn't be hard."

"Yes sir," said STEAM. "Ready."

"Good." Gabriel put on a headset, and he flipped a couple of switches. A series of hums sounded, like a dotted line: *um . . . um . . . um . . .* Through the speaker, a voice said, *"Light Blade* here." Gabriel recognized the voice as Siena's.

He spoke into the headset, using a low, rumbling voice that didn't sound like his own at all, and he left pauses between words, and he threw in some odd little squeaks and scratchy noises. "Clow Lep eer," he said. "Can't . . . *skreek* . . . bad connex . . . *ip, ip, ip* . . . connection . . . *rrrrrooww.* Plz tune yer . . ."

Siena shouted back. "What? Can't hear you!"

Gabriel made a few more strange noises, and at the same time, his fingers were flying over the buttons and switches built into STEAM's controls.

Siena was clearly annoyed. "Who is this? Is there some kind of emergency? I can't hear what you're saying!"

A bright yellow light lit up on STEAM's console. It flashed slowly and steadily. Gabriel grinned. *Got it!* he thought. He was having fun with the weird noises, so he made a few more. *"Ooob-wahg,"* he growled in a low groaning sort of voice, like a motor running down. *"Oooom.* Losing . . . loo-o-o-zing you . . ." And he disconnected.

He jumped up from the pilot's seat. He fiddled again with the buttons on the control, and then he typed in a command and peered at the display. "Right now," he said, "SUMI is in recharge mode. Perfect. We'll do a test run." He pressed the final button.

Piper, bored out of her mind, was playing a video game. She knew that Anna and Ravi had taken off for Tundra by now, with Colin at the helm of the transport ship. That meant that only Niko and

Siena were on board. SUMI had returned from the team meeting and was recharging, which meant no hide-and-seek, nothing happening. The recharging happened several times a day and took twenty minutes or so, during which SUMI was asleep—that is, nonoperational. Piper had at first used these times to explore the training room, looking for a way out, but by now, she'd covered every inch—many times. So there was nothing to do while SUMI recharged but play games. Or take a nap.

The video game was way too simple for her, so she was actually beginning to nod off when she heard a strange voice. It said one word, which sounded like *correction*. She whipped around. SUMI was still plugged in, looking lifeless. So it wasn't SUMI talking. Was someone hiding in here? Piper's heart began to pound. She guided her air chair very slowly toward where she thought she'd heard the voice.

It came again. "Connection," it said, low and robotic. It *was* coming from SUMI! But it wasn't SUMI's voice. Piper approached the little robot warily. "What?"

"Confirm your name," the voice said.

"SUMI, are you okay?" asked Piper.

"Uh . . . yes. Rebooting. Please provide proof of

identity," the voice said. Piper thought she knew that voice, and it wasn't SUMI. "Answer this question: What is the name of the Alpha slogger?"

Now she was sure—it was someone from her team!

Piper knew the answer, of course. "TULIP," she said eagerly.

"Excellent," said the voice. "Petunia is now your code name. Speed Devil Supreme here, also known as Gabe. Press enter if you copy."

Gabe! *Gabriel* was calling! Amazement flooded through her. And joy. She floated next to SUMI, pressed her enter button, and listened.

"Piper, I have a plan! I'm gonna get you out! I need to know SUMI's down times and when she's alone with you."

With shaky fingers, Piper entered the times when SUMI routinely recharged.

"Be ready for messages at those times!" Gabriel said. "Sign on with your code name if you're alone and it's safe to connect."

Piper laughed. "Will do. Just one thing—why do you get to be Speed Devil Supreme and I have to be a flower?"

"Signing off now," said Gabe with a goofy laugh.

There was a quiet beep, and his voice was gone.

Piper let out a whoop and sailed her air chair up to the ceiling and all around the room. There was hope. She was going home! Gabriel had a plan.

9

Carly brought the Streak to a halt beside a drift of snow. Up a slope several yards away was a dark opening in the mountainside. The Omega team's snowmobile was parked in front of it. There was no sign of anyone.

"They can't have been here long," Carly said. "If we'd gotten here just five minutes ago. . . ." She trailed off, but Dash knew what she was thinking. *If he hadn't wasted precious minutes adjusting settings, which he could have done perfectly well while they were moving . . .* He frowned and pushed the thought away. He couldn't help it if she was mad at him. It was better than telling her the truth.

They scrambled out of the Streak and made their way to the cave. Snow had blown into a deep bank at the cave entrance, and boot prints in the snow showed that two Omegas must be inside. Dash and Carly clambered up and over.

Dash turned for a moment to look out at the view from this high place. Vast stretches of snow, dark stone ridges and cliffs, and, far away, some things he couldn't identify. To the northeast, there was a long glint of rippling silver, almost like water, only of course it couldn't be water. And off to the northwest, what looked like a field of gray, like . . . like . . . all he could think of was a parking lot full of gray cars, but that was impossible. Probably it was a field of boulders. And farther away still, the air seemed to shimmer with what looked like vertical clouds.

They came to the mouth of the cave a few steps farther on. Inside, they found themselves in a high, dim space, its walls black and complicated by shadows. Here and there, light gleamed on ice crystals like diamonds embedded in the walls.

They changed frequencies to try to hear the Omega team. They stood still and listened.

Distant voices.

Sounds of footsteps.

The connection wasn't great, but it was clear the Omegas were in the cave.

"Lights," said Dash, and they took their flashlights

from the hooks at their sides, because even though sunlight slanted in through the cave door, they'd soon be beyond its reach.

Chris had told them where to find the Talons—as well as he remembered. It had been a long time since he'd left them here. They would have to go to the back of the first room of the cave, and there they'd find a low passage—so low that they'd have to go through it on their hands and knees. At the end of that passage, they'd find a much larger cavern with a ceiling so high Chris's flashlight hadn't been able to illuminate all of it. This was where the Talons were hidden.

Carly and Dash set out to locate the passage. Voices still sounded faintly in their ears and made them impatient to find the Omegas, but the going was slow. The cave floor was slippery and uneven; luckily, the rubber treads on their boots gripped fairly well. Dash led the way, and they moved farther in, sliding their hands along the wall, running their light beams up and down ahead of them.

Then Carly called out excitedly. "Here, Dash, I think this might be it."

Dash came up beside her. He and Carly shone

their flashlight beams forward and saw a hole in the wall about the size of a small fireplace, a rough half circle of darkness. "Yes, that must be it," Dash said. He lowered his light to the gritty floor. "Look— footsteps."

"Omegas," said Carly. "Unless those are Chris's footsteps from a hundred years ago. Probably not."

Dash stooped down and peered into the hole. "The ceiling's low," he said. "We really are going to have to crawl to go through."

Neither one hesitated. They tucked their flash- lights partway into their pockets so they'd aim for- ward and light the way, and then they dropped to their hands and knees and entered the passage. Carly led this time. Dash raised a hand and felt the cold stone inches above his head.

The passage was several yards long. When it ended, they could feel space opening around them again, and now the voices were coming through more clearly on the radio—it was Anna and Ravi.

"*There* you are!" called Anna. "It took you long enough. We've been here for ages."

Dash looked up and saw a spot of light—the beam of Anna's flashlight. She was halfway up the side of

the cave, high above where he and Carly were. He swept the beam of his own flashlight farther upward and saw that this part of the cave was immense, its ceiling lost in darkness. The walls were wrinkled and cracked, as if made of old leather crushed down by the mountain above. Anna was standing on a ledge that ran at a steep slant from nearly floor level up along the wall. She was holding something under her arm.

Ravi appeared beside Anna. Dash realized there must be an alcove in the wall behind them. Ravi was holding something too.

Dash started toward the ledge.

"No!" shouted Anna. "We're coming down, and the ledge isn't wide enough for us to pass each other. Wait for us where you are."

As they made their way down, Dash followed them with his flashlight beam. He could see how narrow the ledge was, especially for people wearing bulky snowsuits. They inched along slowly, sometimes going sideways, with their backs to the wall.

Anna was the first one down. She came over to them. "We got what we came for," she said. "There were two of them. We'll take both, since we got here first."

"You will *not*," said Dash. He took a step toward Anna. He was trying to stay calm. "If you take both of them and something happens to you—you get lost, or you're buried in an avalanche, or you fall down a crevasse—then they're both gone and the mission has failed."

"That won't happen," Anna said. As she spoke, Ravi jumped down from the ledge behind her, and as he landed next to Anna, he dropped the object he'd been carrying.

Carly darted forward and picked it up as Anna sighed in annoyance. "Really, Ravi?" she said. "Having a clumsy day?"

"Sorry," said Ravi.

Dash turned his flashlight on the object.

"I thought it would be more like a knife," said Carly.

"I didn't think it would be so strange-looking," said Ravi.

"It's an alien instrument," said Dash. "I guess we should expect it to be strange." He held his hands out. "Let me see."

Carly handed it to him.

Dash could see right away why Chris called

it the Talon. It was nearly a foot long, a spike of silver-gray steel, and as thin and scaly as a hawk's leg. At one end was a double claw—a talon—whose points were so sharp that Dash was sure that if you touched one even lightly it would draw blood.

At the other end was a sort of handle. He looked more closely at it and saw that it was actually a small oval container, about the size of a box for a piece of jewelry or a retainer. It was made of gleaming metal, a coppery color. On either side of it was a handle of the same reddish-gold metal, and on the top was a symbol inlaid in silver—a spiral with a tiny star at the center. It was a beautiful thing, and frightening too.

Dash understood how it would be. *We'll have to stand very close to the ice crawler,* he thought. *We'll grip the box by its handles and run that claw down the crawler's skin, with just the right pressure to draw the crystals into the box. If it doesn't work, we'll have to start over and do it again. And the ice crawler will be—doing what?*

No one spoke for a moment.

Then Anna lunged toward Dash. "Give it back," she said, but her voice wasn't as firm as before.

"No," said Dash. "You have one; we have one.

We have a better chance of getting some of those crystals if we've got two teams going after them."

"You still seem to think we're all in this together," Anna said.

"Of course I do."

Anna shrugged. "The strongest team will finish the mission first," she said. "It makes a difference which team that is. I know it's us."

Carly couldn't contain her anger. "If you're so strong, why did you need to kidnap Piper? That's not a strong move—that's weak and underhanded!"

She took a step toward Anna, but Dash grabbed her arm. "We don't have time for this," he said. "We have to find an ice crawler and get the job done."

"You're right, for once," said Anna. "Let's go, Ravi. We're out of here."

The two of them turned around and made their way toward the low passage. Carly and Dash followed, and when they came out of the cave, they saw Anna and Ravi standing by their vehicle, looking uncertainly at a silvery spiral towering over the landscape to the north.

"Some kind of storm," said Ravi. "Looks cyclone-ish."

They watched. It came closer, rose higher,

seemed to bend toward them, took up more and more of the sky.

"I say we go anyhow," Anna announced. "Quick, Rav, get in the Cheetah. We'll cut through it, or circle around it. We'll be all right."

This storm looked different and possibly worse than the one that had toppled the Streak. "I don't think it's safe," Dash said.

"If you don't take risks," said Anna, "you don't win success."

"But if you take too many risks, or bad ones," said Dash, "you don't win anything. You end up wrecked or dead."

"*We* don't," Anna said. "You're thinking of *your* team. Come on, Ravi, let's go."

Ravi glanced uneasily at the oncoming funnel-shaped cloud, and then he cast a worried look at Dash and Carly. But he followed Anna to the vehicle, and they got in, roared the engine, and sped away into the endless white.

Dash watched them go. They were being stupid, he thought. Typical Anna. Too focused on winning to think about her safety or her team's. No—it took some courage to head into that storm. Maybe she was right about risk.

On the other hand, that storm could tear them to pieces.

But if it didn't, they'd have a huge head start.

The shimmering funnel cloud was coming at them fast, enormous at the top and narrow at the bottom, like a giant hand with a finger scraping over the ground. The Omega vehicle traced a wide curve around it, shrinking into a dot as it got farther away.

"We can't let them get so far ahead," said Carly.

Dash knew all at once that he felt the same. "No," he said, "we can't." And they sprinted—as much as they could in knee-deep drifts—for the Streak.

10

In the *Cloud Leopard* training room, Gabriel started in on the next step of his rescue mission. "Time to work, STEAM," he said, and STEAM shuffled over to him. "Ready to work, yes sir."

"I just need to get your send-and-receive function going here"—he pressed some buttons—"and plug into the *Light Blade* network"—he entered some numbers, his fingers flying over STEAM's console—"and let's check that list Piper sent."

There on the screen was the list of the times when SUMI recharged herself. The next one wasn't for forty-five minutes. That was too long to wait.

"Have to work on this a little more," Gabriel said to STEAM. He bent over the keys. "Got to take over the robot's system. That means . . ." As fast

as he could, he entered some code. "And then . . ."
More quick typing. "Okay. Let's see if that works."

He reached for the headset and put it on. Holding
down the intersystem switch, he said, "Come in,
Petunia. Do you hear me?"

At first, there was nothing but a scratchy silence.

"Calling Petunia," Gabe said. "Petunia! Urgent!"

And the answer came back in an eager voice.
"Petunia here!"

"Tell me where you are."

"Training room. Locked in. SUMI has the code
for the door."

With the touch of a couple of buttons, Gabriel
downloaded the plans of the *Light Blade* and
scanned them to check the location of the training
room. "Perfect," he said. "We can make this rescue
happen. Can't talk now, but I'll get in touch soon,
next time SUMI is charging. I'm going to tell you
exactly what to do."

In the library of the *Light Blade,* Niko was sitting at the
table he liked best, the one in the corner farthest from
the door. He came to the library sometimes when he
needed a relief from the regular routine. Niko loved

adventure stories the most. Right now, he had *Disaster on Wreckage Island* on the screen in front of him.

He wasn't exactly reading, however. He was staring at the page, his elbows on the table and his chin in his hands. He was having an argument in his mind.

Am I being disloyal?

No, this is the right thing to do.

But what if it made everything worse?

Still, I can't really—

It was an argument he'd had several times in the last few days. He couldn't make up his mind, and it was driving him crazy. He kept nibbling on his fingernails, as if that would help.

"Niko." It was a sharp whisper, coming from behind him. He whirled around and saw Siena. She must have been reading in the far back corner, sitting behind the high stack of humming servers that held thousands of books and movies in digital form.

"What are you doing?" she said. "You haven't moved for fifteen minutes. There can't be one page that's so fascinating." She came and stood behind him. "*Wreckage Island?*" she read over his shoulder. "I hope that's not research."

"No, not research," Niko said. "Not even reading. Just thinking." He knew it was time for him to talk with Siena. They had both been feeling the same thing: that they didn't like the way Colin and Anna were leading the Omega team.

For Niko, the trick Anna had played on Piper was the last straw. It seemed cruel. And why was it necessary? Having a prisoner from the Alpha team wouldn't make their own team any better. They already had a perfectly good medic—him! It was true that as long as the *Light Blade* had Piper on board, the Alpha team wouldn't desert the Omega team when the time came to go into Gamma Speed. But he didn't really think they would desert the *Light Blade* anyhow. Stealing Piper just made no sense to him.

But if he spoke out against Anna and Colin, what would happen? How would it do any good? What he'd really like to do was quit Omega and join the Alpha team. But Anna would flip out. And now that his team had kidnapped Piper, he doubted the Alphas would take him anyway.

Siena came around the table and sat down across from him. She was thinking about the whispers that had passed between them. A couple of times after Colin had given a harsh order, Niko had murmured to Siena, "*That* didn't seem necessary." Or after Anna had said something impatient or unkind, Niko had shot Siena a quick look that said *I don't like this*. And then, once the *Clipper* had left for Tundra, they'd agreed that they had to make a plan.

Now was the time. "Listen," Siena said quietly. "I've had it with Omega. I think you have too."

Niko nodded. Relief flooded through him. Having Siena on his side made a huge difference. He told her that she was right: he was also unhappy about the way things were going. "Especially," he said, "about having a prisoner."

"I know," Siena said. "I was thinking. We could let her out of the training room."

"Right," Niko agreed, switching off his reading screen. "But then what?"

"We could hide her somewhere and tell Anna we'd taken her hostage. We'd tell her why—that we really don't like what's happening with the team."

"For lots of reasons," Niko added. "Not only because of Piper."

"Yes. And what about this: we say we won't tell

her where Piper is until she agrees to make some changes."

Niko shook his head. "It would never work. She'd just search the whole ship until she found her."

"But what if we gave her a deadline?" Siena leaned forward, her eyes burning with excitement. "Make some changes by six this evening, or else we'll find a way to get Piper home."

Niko's eyes went wide. "That would be mutiny," he said. "Anna would be furious. Colin would too. They'd probably grab us and lock us in the training room along with Piper."

"They can't," said Siena. "They need us."

"Do they?" Niko said. "Sometimes it seems like Anna would rather be on this mission alone."

Siena nodded. "Yeah . . . but if they were down two team members, things would get a whole lot harder. Like it or not, Anna needs help."

"Okay, but how would we get Piper home? If it comes to that?"

"How did she get over here? Doesn't she have a jetpack or something?" Siena asked.

Niko's eyebrows went up. "I think she does."

"Do you know where it is?"

"No, but I bet we can find out. We can start by asking her."

"She might not know."

"Or she might. We won't know until we ask." Niko stood up. "Let's do it." He smiled. "I think Piper's lunch is going to come a little early today."

They zoomed through the maze to the kitchen. ZRKs were hard at work there, opening bottles and packets, measuring out powders and liquids, stirring things that bubbled in pots.

"Hey, ZRKs," said Niko. The buzzing and fluttering stopped for a second. ZRKs hovered, listening. "We need lunch a little early for our prisoner. Like right now. Can you do it?"

They could. The little robots got speedier, and their buzzing got louder, and in under three minutes they had a tray of quite delicious-looking food ready to go.

"Thanks!" Niko said, taking the tray, and he and Siena hurried down the hall.

Coming right toward them, moving with a purposeful stride, was Colin.

"What's going on?" he demanded.

Niko tried not to look as dismayed as he felt. Incredible bad luck! He'd thought Colin would have gone to his quarters when he got back from taking the team to Tundra. "Lunch for our captive," he said lightly.

Colin checked the time. "Over an hour early?" he said. "Some reason for that?"

Niko's mind went blank, but Siena filled in for him. She looked at her MTB and gave a small yelp of surprise. "Whoa, you're right, Colin!" she said. "Niko, we must have read the time wrong. Sorry!"

Colin frowned at them. "You two are falling down on the job lately," he said. "Get your act together. There's no room for sloppiness on this ship." He glared at them. His glance fell to the tray Niko was holding. "And we don't waste food either," he said. "I'll find a use for this." He took the tray and stood there scowling at them until they turned around and walked away.

When he was gone, Niko said, "Guess what he's going to do with that food."

"Eat it himself," said Siena.

"Right." Niko sighed. "Bad luck for our plan, but we'll try again later."

Siena nodded. "After Colin goes back to Tundra to pick up the team."

"Perfect," Niko said. "All Piper will have to do is tell us where that jetpack is, and we'll get her out of there."

11

Dash and Carly wrenched open the doors of the Streak. Sharp-edged snowflakes came at them in fierce gusts of icy wind. They crammed themselves inside and buckled their straps. Far off in the distance, the Omega Cheetah vanished into the coming storm.

Dash set the Talon in the back with TULIP, bracing it behind the box of emergency supplies so it wouldn't bounce around and stab someone, and Carly started the motor. It growled once, twice, and roared to life.

"Heat signature at forty-six degrees east, eight degrees north of us," said Dash. "Let's not follow Anna. If we curve around the storm to the right instead, it looks like we might get to a herd faster."

"Okay. We'll do it." Carly pressed the accelerator. In seconds, she'd pushed the Streak up to full speed.

Once again, they bounded over the rough terrain through swirls of white, bumping, soaring, rocking from side to side—but this time the storm was different. Through the whirling flakes, they could see a towering column ahead and slightly to the right of them, and even over the racket of the Streak's motor, they could hear the high, shrill sound of the wind. There was a strange twittering quality to the sound, as if it were made up of a million separate pieces.

"Farther left!" Dash shouted.

Carly steered left, up a bank that tilted the Streak steeply, but their speed held them and they zoomed on over uneven ground that had TULIP bouncing in the back, making small croaking sounds of distress. The whirling vortex swerved away from them, then changed direction and came toward them. It looked thick, as though it had sucked in all the snowflakes from miles around.

"Something up ahead!" Dash yelled, pointing. "And another one right behind it!"

Carly saw them—big solid balls of whiteness hurtling down a slope through the storm. She steered frantically away, avoiding the snowballs but veering closer to the point of the whirlwind, which was moving faster than the Streak could go. "I can't outrun it!" Carly shouted. "It's going to catch us!"

She felt the wind pulling at them like a magnet, sucking the Streak into a curve no matter how hard she tried to hold it straight. Then, to her horror, the front tips of the runners began to rise from the ground.

"It's lifting us up!" she cried.

The Streak tilted. Dash and Carly were thrown backward in their seats. The Streak rose and turned, and they saw that they were caught low on the inside of an enormous funnel, circling the narrow part, but with each circle going up farther toward the wide part, a foot off the ground, two feet, higher and higher . . . Outside the windshield, the world went white, as if a sheet had been thrown across the glass. They were in the center of a whirlwind.

All the engine power in the world wouldn't help them now. The wind would spiral them to the top and fling them out into the sky. *We're done for,* Dash thought.

But no. They were only about three feet off the ground when the funnel suddenly blew apart, exploding into flakes that filled the air. The whirling column had dissolved into millions of insects fluttering like snow to the ground. In minutes, the white of the snow was covered with a vast carpet of white glitter.

The Streak crashed down and landed on its runners, with its engine still going. Carly stamped on the brakes, and it skidded and veered sideways. Dash grabbed the door handle. He felt a jolt as TULIP banged into his seat back. The door on Carly's side flew open, and instantly the air was thick with a buzzing, chittering, flickering swarm.

"Bugs!" Dash hollered. He batted them away from his face.

Carly stretched out, caught the door handle, and heaved the door closed. The insects in the cab hurled themselves against the glass, against the walls, against Carly's and Dash's helmets, against TULIP—tap-tap-tap-tappity-tap-tappity-tap—until finally they fell to the floor in heaps, stunned or dead.

"Snow locusts," said Dash, wiping his glove across the front of his helmet. "It's not a whirlwind; it's a bug blizzard."

Carly plucked a dead locust from her sleeve.

"Hideous," she said, "but interesting. Look." She held it up. When Chris had said *locusts,* they both had pictured a grasshopper-like insect, with back legs bent upward over a long, narrow body. But this thing was shaped like a fat little bullet, pure silver-white and shiny as a refrigerator door. Its wings were transparent, and its head was nothing but a bump equipped with a set of tiny teeth. It wasn't really an insect at all—it had eight legs, like a spider, not six—and the legs were short and thick, nothing but stubs with a couple of tiny claws at the end of each one.

"Ick," said Carly. "Locusts are crunchy. These are squishy."

Dozens still clung to Dash's clothes. With a shudder, he brushed them off. Outside, the ground seethed with them.

"These are what the ice crawlers eat," Dash said.

"Right," said Carly. "So if there's a swarm of snow locusts around, we might see an ice crawler too."

"I bet we already did see some!" Dash said. "Those snowballs rolling down the slope. They must have been crawlers collecting dinner."

"Let's go find one that isn't in the middle of

a bug storm." Carly pressed the start button. The motor sputtered, but the Streak didn't move. She tried again. Still nothing. "Something's clogged the engine," she said.

They looked at each other. "Locusts," said Dash.

Less than a mile away, the herd of crawlers moved forward a little faster now, sensing both the strange intruder and also the definite smell of food. It was a loose and disorganized herd. It had no leader. Often a single crawler or a small group would wander off, losing track of the others.

A couple of them were doing that just now, gliding up a hill away from the herd, confused by the different smells in the air, knowing only that somewhere nearby was something good to eat and that they should get ready. One of them reared up to get a better look at the landscape, lifting its front end twenty feet in the air and exposing its long slit of a mouth. It made a hiss like a snake's, only far louder. Other crawlers around it did the same, until the herd came to look like a forest of thick, pale trees, swaying weirdly.

12

At least it was warm inside the stalled Streak, thanks to TULIP, whose tummy glowed cozily red. Dash was tempted to sit there for a while and catch his breath, but he couldn't let himself do that. The Streak's pipes had to be cleared, or they'd be stuck and their mission would be over. "Here I go," he told Carly.

He opened the door and stepped outside.

It was as if his clothes turned instantly to sheets of ice pressing against his skin. His joints stiffened; he could hardly move. He took a long breath and slowly got down on his knees. He fumbled for his flashlight, got it unhooked, and aimed it down the Streak's intake pipe. There it was—a messy glob of snow locusts, as if the pipe had been stuffed with mashed potatoes.

Dash took his knife from its sheath on his belt. The blade wasn't very long, so he had to put more than half his arm into the pipe to reach the clog. He poked and scraped and pulled the mess toward him. Clumps of it fell out onto the snow and onto his boots. Finally, he thought he'd gotten it all— and then he heard Carly's voice over the radio.

"Dash! A heat signal! Close!"

He took a quick look at his mobile tech. Yes, *really* close. He stood up and scanned the landscape. It was hard to see very far, because stray locusts were still fluttering in the air like snowflakes. But after a few seconds, he spotted it. "There!" he shouted, pointing at the base of a hill several hundred yards away. A large oval object showed against the white. "It has to be an ice crawler!" Dash called to Carly.

He gave the tailpipe one last scrape with his knife and hurried back inside. Carly hit the start button— and the engine made a choking sound and died.

"Try again!" Dash cried. "I thought I got that pipe cleared!"

Again, Carly pressed start. "Come on, come on," she urged. The engine coughed with a noise like a throat clearing, but the Streak didn't move. There must still be locusts in the tailpipe.

ZRK PROBE DATA | PLANET TUNDRA

TOP-SECRET MISSION BRIEF

LIGHT BLADE | PERSONNEL

FIRST NAME	Ike	LAST NAME	Phillips
AGE AT-TIME OF ENLISTMENT		65	
GENDER	M	DATE OF BIRTH	Unknown
NATION OF ORIGIN		United States of America	
NEXT OF KIN		Shawn Phillips, son—estranged	
CURRENT LOCATION		Unknown	
TITLE/POSITION		Dishonorably discharged from Project Alpha; current Omega base leader	

LIGHT BLADE—RECON DATA

FIRST NAME	SUMI	AGE	Manufactured six months ago
ACRONYM		Sentient Universal Mechanical Instructor	
MANUFACTURER		"Omega Base"	
POSITION/TITLE		A.I. consultant, onboard training robot	
DUTIES		Hide-and-go-seek, astronomic calculus	

Dash had to make a fast decision: try again to clear the pipe, or risk the cold and run toward the crawler on foot? What if this crawler was the only one within miles? They might not get another chance.

"We have to get out and run," he said.

Carly nodded and pushed open the door.

Dash reached behind the seat and grabbed the Talon, and then he too climbed back out into the cold. Although the vortex had dissolved, hundreds of locusts still flittered around in the air. It would have been easy to get lost in this white wilderness. But he could still make out a solid shape through the fluttering, and he made his way toward it, with Carly following. After a few minutes, he pulled his binoculars from their pouch and focused in.

What he saw sent a jolt through him. The oval shape was not an ice crawler.

"Carly!" he yelled into his radio. "It's the Omega team's snowmobile up ahead! They're already here!" He felt a wave of fury—how could he and Carly be *losing* this race?—but he stamped it down. Not useful to spend energy on anger.

Again he put the binoculars to his eyes. This time he saw what he hadn't noticed before, because it was white against white: there was a very large ball of snow a short distance away from the snowmobile. He radioed Carly again. "There *is* a crawler! Their team is right up next to it!"

"Okay," Carly said. "I hate that they found it first, but it doesn't really matter. We can both take zero crystals from this one. Let's get there."

They plowed on through the drifts as fast as they could. The going was slow, not just because of the cold and wind but also because they were walking uphill. The Omega snowmobile and the crawler stood about halfway up a long, smooth slope that rose to a peak up above them. Dash struggled to control a jaw-cracking shiver. Whoever had designed the protective suits they were wearing had never been on the planet Tundra. These suits might have worked fine on Antarctica, or the frozen Siberian plains. Here, they felt like barely more than a fleece.

Up ahead, through his binoculars, he saw Anna and Ravi getting out of the Cheetah and approaching the locust ball cautiously.

"That ball is huge, all right," Dash said to Carly. "Their vehicle looks small beside it."

Carly was looking too. "An *elephant* would look small beside it," she said.

They struggled on. They were close now. The wind was like a powerful ocean current they had to struggle against. They leaned forward, forcing themselves on, their boots plunging into deep snow with every step. Dash's feet were numb. His fingers were too, even inside the thickly padded gloves.

"Look!" cried Carly. "It's coming out!"

Dash clapped his binocs to his eyes again. Yes— the crawler was eating its way out of the ball of bugs. He stood still and watched as something white rose through the writhing insects like a mushroom pushing up through the snow, shedding clumps and splinters of ice. It didn't look like any sort of animal Dash recognized—not a bear or ape, not a worm or snake, not a giant lizard or spider or other crawling thing. He couldn't see if it had a face or even a head. It seemed to be simply a massive grayish-white lump. He saw Anna and Ravi stumble backward, looking at it.

The creature unfolded itself, and Dash could see that its shape kept shifting slightly, bulging out in one spot and then another, the way a balloon does when it's filled with water.

"It's sort of like a huge seal," said Carly, staring.

"Or a giant walrus," said Dash.

The crawler suddenly heaved its front part up from the ground, revealing a grayish underside. Dash focused in closer, toward a spot where there was a white flutter of locusts, and something moving within it. It was a mouth—a hole in the crawler's skin. It opened and closed as if controlled by a drawstring. Open, it sucked in a thick stream of snow locusts. Closed, it shrank to a puckered bump, and bits of chewed locust dribbled down from it.

"Does it have legs?" Carly said to Dash.

"I can't tell," he called back. He couldn't take his eyes from that horrible mouth, growing wide and shrinking down. He glimpsed flashing, knife-like teeth within it.

After several seconds, he saw that the eating was slowing, and the ice crawler seemed to be growing shorter and wider, bulging out sideways. The mouth stopped moving, and the crawler lowered its front half slowly, until it spread out like a huge slug on the ground and lay still. *That's the coma,* Dash thought—the deep after-dinner sleep.

They were only about fifty feet away now. Dash

raised both arms and waved, hoping Anna would wait until they got there so they could all approach the crawler together.

But Anna had other ideas. She held the Talon with both hands. She got up close to the crawler. Hesitantly, she touched its side with her foot.

It shuddered, like a great mound of Jell-O.

"She's going to do the extraction," Dash called over the radio.

"I know," said Carly. "So are we, if she doesn't chase the thing away."

Anna stood beside the creature. Its body rose in front of her like a hill. She raised the Talon.

Dash held his breath. Would it rear up at her touch and attack?

But it didn't move, and Anna seemed to gain confidence. Ravi was close behind her now, ready to help if necessary.

"Here she goes," said Dash.

Anna steadied herself, raised the Talon, and brought the spike down with great speed, scraping it along the ice crawler's flesh. Dash cringed. He was sure she did it much harder than she needed to. Chris had said that it would take hardly more than a scratch to do it and that the crawler might not even notice.

But this one did notice. The big body twitched, and the crawler made a sound—a low, sad moan, like the moo of a cow.

Anna jumped back. She and Ravi started toward their Cheetah, and Anna turned to flash a triumphant look straight at Dash. It said *We did it. We beat you.*

Then came another sound, much louder. It came from the top of the peak, and it was so tremendous that Dash felt the ground shake beneath his feet. It was a bellow, a huge, rumbling roar. He saw Anna look up, and he looked up too, and at once, he understood that the ice crawler Anna had stabbed was not really that huge at all.

It was a baby.

And that had to be its mother, up above. She was beyond enormous.

Anna and Ravi froze in horror for a second. The immense crawler moved toward them. They raced to the Cheetah, and Dash heard the scream of its engine as it sped away.

Carly's voice, very quiet, came through the transmitter. "What do we do?"

Dash's first thought was to go for it. They might not find other crawlers. It could be that Anna hadn't got the zero crystals, even though she had tried. If that were true and he and Carly didn't get crystals from this crawler, the Tundra mission would be a failure. And that meant their *entire* mission would be a failure.

But then he saw the mother crawler coming over the crest of the hill. With remarkable speed, she slid down toward her calf. Dash could see her tail now, T-shaped like a whale's, slapping against the snow behind her. Just as she reached her baby, she seemed to notice Dash and Carly standing there in the snow a few dozen feet away. Her huge sides rippled in and out. Her body seemed to swell forward.

"She's coming at us," Dash said.

"She's going to see us," Carly said. "If those red eyes can see."

And sure enough, the creature turned toward them and began surging in their direction, picking up speed. There was not a moment to spare.

"Back to the Streak!" Dash yelled.

They turned and ran.

13

Piper sat in her air chair in the *Light Blade* training room, watching SUMI update the tension levels of some of the workout machines. A swarm of ZRKs buzzed around her, oiling and dusting and polishing. Piper was in a fury of impatience. Now that she knew Gabe could communicate with her, she couldn't wait for SUMI's recharging sessions. The next one was still forty minutes away. Piper was sure she was going to die of suspense.

She tried to focus her mind. The ZRKs distracted her, fluttering their tiny polishing rags, twittering and chattering in their squeaky, birdlike way. Such strange little creatures, no bigger than golf balls and yet capable of doing so many useful tasks . . .

And thinking about strange creatures made

her think about Tundra, and that made her long to know what kinds of creatures were down there and how her team was doing—she couldn't *stand* not knowing! They'd be tromping around on Tundra right now! And how were things going back on the *Cloud Leopard*, her ship that she missed so much? How was their dog, Rocket? She yanked the control stick of the air chair, sped up toward the ceiling, and zoomed around in furious circles. It was *awful* not to know.

The ZRKs seemed to sense that she was upset. A bunch of them swarmed up and surrounded her air chair, tapping it all over, chattering like mad, trying to fix her. "I'm fine, I'm fine!" Piper protested, batting at them, but one of them buzzed in her ear and another one tangled itself in her hair until she screamed, "Get away!" and they finally flew off.

She had to calm herself. Being upset only made things worse; she knew that. So she parked her air chair by the Alien Commando Warships video game and was about to start playing it for the thousandth incredibly boring time, when she heard something that made her hand fly off the joystick.

It was Gabriel's voice.

She whipped around. She saw that SUMI, who had been humming along busily just a moment before, was frozen mid-action. Gabe's voice was coming through her.

"Speed Devil here. Come in, Petunia. Are you there?"

Piper sped to SUMI. "I'm here!" she whispered.

"Took over SUMI's system," said Gabe. "No time to wait for recharging. Need to give you instructions."

"I'm ready!"

"Okay. Right now, I'm scanning SUMI's code to find the bit that unlocks the door. Stand by."

Piper stood by—or rather, sat by. Her heart was going fast—she measured her heart rate, just to have something to do. Pulse of ninety-one. Super fast. She was about to get *out* of here!

She heard Gabe muttering to himself. "If this is . . . but then where's . . . hmmm." He spoke again. "Pretty dense piece of programming here," he said. "But I think I've got it. This should open the door."

"Tell me!"

"But wait, Piper. I have to explain the plan for when you get out of the training room."

Piper couldn't bear to wait. "I want to try the

door!" she said. "Right now! Give me the numbers. I have to see if it works, I'll just open the door and close it right up again. Then you can tell me the rest."

"You're sure no one's out in the hall?"

"I'm sure! Lunch isn't for another half hour at least!"

"Okay. Try this: on the console, press zero-zero and then a capital T-R and then enter three-star-eight-star-nine-six-four."

Piper hovered over the blinking lights of the SUMI control panel. She followed Gabe's directions. Press here, press there, enter numbers. Then she zipped to the door and waited. A few clicks sounded from the lock mechanism. Then a sort of clunk. Then nothing.

She waited.

The door stayed closed. "It didn't work!" she told him.

"Don't worry," he said. "I'll keep trying. Back to you soon."

In the training room with STEAM by his side, Gabe roamed through the intricacies of SUMI's brain. Whoever had written these programs had been a weird kind of genius, he thought. He kept running into complex loops and clever cryptics. It was a real puzzle. Huddling over the screen was giving him a pain in the neck, but he had to keep at it. The Tundra team would be ready for pickup around one thirty, unless they were delayed. To be safe, he'd tell Piper to be ready for rescue at one. He could surely have the *Cloud Cat* back in time for the Tundra pickup.

Behind him came the sound of footsteps. He was startled for a moment, and then relaxed. It wasn't the thump of human feet. It was the tap-tap of dog feet. Rocket came up alongside him and pressed his head against Gabe's leg.

"Hi, boy," Gabe said. "What's going on?"

Rocket looked up at him with his shining brown eyes. He gave a couple of quick little barks, like questions.

Gabe scratched Rocket's ears. "Okay," he said. "I'll play with you. But I have to get this job done first. Can you wait about five minutes?"

Rocket sighed and lay down on the floor.

"Good dog," said Gabriel. He went back to studying SUMI's programming. In several places, he saw the word *trngrm*, which must mean "training room." He also saw the word *lock* here and there. If he could just figure out what this line meant and how it connected to that line . . .

He worked at it a few minutes longer and came up with three possibilities. He couldn't tell which—if any—might be right.

He spoke into the transmitter. "Petunia, are you still there?" I have new codes for you to try."

"Ready," Piper spoke into the transmitter. She was on fire with eagerness.

Gabriel read out the string of numbers and letters and symbols. Piper entered them on SUMI's console. As before, the door's lock made a couple of clicking sounds but stayed firmly closed.

"Okay, here's the second one," said Gabriel.

Piper's finger was poised over the keyboard. But at that moment, there was a knock at the training room door. Rap-rappa-rap-rap. The meal-time knock. But it wasn't lunchtime, was it? Piper checked the clock—she was right. Why were they bringing lunch early?

Piper froze. A voice called, "SUMI! Where are you? Open up!"

It was Siena's voice.

Piper whispered frantically to Gabriel. "Wait! Don't say anything."

"Why—"

"*Ssshh!*" Piper hissed.

Again came the knock on the door. "SUMI!" This time it was Niko's voice.

SUMI, nonoperational for the moment, didn't respond.

Piper held her breath. *Go away, go away,* she said silently.

Many seconds went by. At last, the knocks and the voices stopped. Piper waited a few more seconds. "Okay," she said to Gabriel. "I think they've left."

"What's going on?" he asked.

"Early lunch, for some reason. Now tell me!"

He read her the second code.

She tried it out. Click. Click. Clatter-clatter. She heard the lock snap open.

She didn't open the door, though. What if Niko and Siena were still out there? She dashed back to the console and whispered, "It worked."

Gabe cheered, but quietly. They had to be careful now and work fast. "Okay, Piper," he said. "First, lock the door again so no one knows you can open it. Just run the same code, only backward."

Piper did this, and she heard the lock clunk into place.

"Done."

Gabe went on. "Here's the main thing: timing is going to be crucial. You have to get out without being seen by SUMI or anyone else. You have to get yourself to the *Light Blade* engine room. And you have to be there by thirteen hundred hours. Can you do that?"

"Yes. Then what?"

"Then you wait. At exactly thirteen hundred hours, I will be there in the *Cloud Cat*. You'll be able to see me from the rear window. As soon as you do, open the outer landing dock door. That should be easy—it looks like it should work the same way as the one on the *Cloud Leopard*. I'll be there with the transport ship."

"Okay," Piper said.

"When you hear me come in," Gabe went on, "open the inner door. After that, you just hop in and I take you back home."

Piper said, "Yaaaay!" Excitement surged through her. Her voice rose to a happy shout. *"I'll be there!"*

"See you soon," said Gabe, and he disconnected.

SUMI jerked awkwardly once or twice. "Temporary malfunction," she said. "Running program check."

Piper looked at the clock again. She had thirty-seven minutes to wait before she could make her break for freedom.

14

Slipping in the snow, tumbling down and rising again in an instant, slapping waist-high drifts out of their way, Dash and Carly ran for the Streak. The ice crawler, made for snow travel, came after them. It was fifty feet away, forty feet, closer and closer.

The Streak was just ahead now. They reached it, flung the doors open, and jumped in. Carly hit the start button—and the engine made a choking sound and died.

"Try again!" Dash cried. "I got that pipe cleared!"

Outside, the ice crawler came closer, humping up and thinning out, like a strange sort of whale dipping and rising through a vast white sea. It slithered forward, not with the smooth glide of a snake but by bulging and stretching, hauling itself across the snow at a speed amazingly fast for such a great monstrous blob of a thing.

Again, Carly pressed start. "Come on, come on," she urged. The engine coughed, but still the Streak didn't move.

And then the ice crawler was upon them, right beside the passenger window. It swelled itself up into a great wobbly mound, thirty feet tall at least, with its tail thrashing and its mouth gaping. Its shadow fell across the Streak and darkened the light inside.

Dash shouted, "Get off! Get away from us!" He could hear the thick glass top creaking in its frame. The crawler's gray-white skin pressed against it, inches from Dash's face.

Carly jabbed at the start button. The engine caught for a second and then choked.

The crawler shoved the Streak with its whole body, full force, and the Streak tipped toward the slope and rolled over, leaving Carly and Dash upside down for a moment before it rolled again. It landed farther down the slope, upright—but the glass top had cracked and flipped off.

"Our roof!" cried Carly. "Can we get it back on?"

"I don't think so," said Dash. "Look at it."

The glass top lay in the snow, broken into three pieces.

They were in the cold. They had no time to feel it, though. Carly jammed a finger on the start button. "Come on, Streak!" Dash yelled, looking out at the ice crawler oozing toward them down the bank. "Go, go, go!"

And finally, the intake pipe sucked in the last of the mashed locusts, the engine caught and roared, the ice crawler fell back, and Carly steered them sharp to the left, up through the drifts, and away.

Escape! It felt terrific for the first ten seconds, and then they understood their danger: they were out in the open now, going at high speed, exposed to the killing cold of Tundra. They could feel it deep in their bones.

"We'll head for the cave," said Carly through clenched teeth. "We can last ten minutes, can't we?"

Dash didn't answer. He didn't know.

He twisted around in his seat and looked behind. He could still see the ice crawler, like a hill in the distance. Was it following them? They were outrunning it.

"How are your hands?" He radioed to Carly as they skimmed over the snow. His own hands were both completely numb. He couldn't have held on to a steering wheel at all.

"Pretty much gone," Carly said back. "I'm holding on with my arms."

Dash knew how frostbite worked. The cold would freeze skin first, but the longer you were exposed to it, the deeper the freeze would go—down into the flesh, the blood vessels, the nerves. Small parts like toes and fingers could freeze all the way through. Mountain climbers in places not nearly this cold ended up losing toes and fingers all the time.

If it hadn't been for TULIP, they might have turned into blocks of ice immediately. But she stood close behind the two front seats, radiating heat from her belly. A lot of that heat was swept away by the freezing wind, but even a little heat was better than none.

"We have to get there fast," Carly said. "Into the cave, out of the wind."

So they flew across the frozen landscape, half out of control. The distance to the cave wasn't far, but after about five minutes, Carly took her foot off the accelerator. "I have to stop," she said. "I can't hold on."

Dash saw that her whole body was shaking with shivers. "Can you move? Get out the door? We'll trade places, I'll drive."

She nodded but didn't speak.

Dash opened the door on his side and swung his boots onto the ground. On numb feet that felt like wood, he stumbled to the other side of the Streak and helped Carly out of the driver's seat and over to the passenger seat. She slumped against the door. He strapped her in and struggled around the snowmobile again, wind howling past his helmet, pelting him with beads of ice.

In the driver's seat, he placed his hands for a moment on TULIP's stomach. It was a while before the heat got through his gloves and warmed his fingers enough so he could feel them. Then he turned TULIP and aimed her heat mostly at Carly. He took hold of the controls.

"Red button," Carly mumbled. "Pedal on right side."

He saw how it worked, and in a minute, they

were speeding forward again. But he was so cold. The wind was roaring in his ears—a strange, deep, uneven roar. The part of him that was alive had dwindled down to a small spark.

"We're weaving!" Carly shouted. "What's wrong? Should I take over again?"

Dash tightened his grip on the steering wheel and got the Streak on a steady path.

Carly looked back, and Dash heard her take a sharp breath. "That one crawler is still following us," she said.

"How close?" asked Dash.

Carly got out her binoculars. "I can't tell," she said. "Stop for just a minute."

Dash brought the Streak to a halt.

The creature was moving. Not fast, but it was still creeping along in the same direction.

"About half a mile. It's still on our tail," Carly said.

Dash let up on the brakes, and the Streak leapt forward. "We'll be safe in the cave," he said.

He drove at top speed, and within five minutes, they'd reached the familiar slope and the mountainside where the mouth of the cave gaped. Dash steered up the slope and brought the Streak to a halt.

It took them some struggle to get TULIP out of the cargo hold; she was small, but she was heavy and her shape made it awkward to get a grip on her—especially with frozen fingers. They each took one side. "Now heave!" Dash cried, but she slipped from their padded gloves and slammed down into a snowbank on her back, squealing, paddling her short legs in the air.

"Let's drag her," said Carly. So they got their arms under her trapezoid head, hoisted, and hauled, carving a deep rut in the snow as they forced their way toward the cave against a wall of wind.

They stumbled inside, where they leaned against a wall, breathing hard. "We'll rest here for a few minutes and warm up," Dash said.

"Right." Carly was nearly too cold to speak.

"Then we'll go out and get the job done," Dash said.

"Yes," Carly murmured. She thought of that herd of creatures moving toward them. They'd have to single one out somehow, and then get close to it, and then . . . She closed her eyes. She'd think about it later. Right now, she was too tired.

About a quarter of a mile away, the mother crawler butted up against the clear, curved, crustlike things that looked like ice but weren't. The crusts had come off the very fast animal that had carried away the two smaller animals. The tracks of this fast animal led out across the snow, making a smooth path, easy to travel on. The ice crawler, with her calf behind her, slid along it.

Farther to the north, Anna and Ravi were still putting distance between themselves and the monstrous ice crawler Anna had scraped with the Talon. They'd been going full speed for several minutes, shaken by their close call, but now the panic was fading.

"Hey," said Ravi. "We did the deed!"

"We did," said Anna, smiling. "Mission accomplished."

"And on the first try!" Ravi added.

"And without accidents or injuries," said Anna.

"Time to check our position," Anna said. "We need to signal Colin to come and get us."

Ravi looked at the GPS on his wrist tech. "Looks to me like we're too far east," he said.

"Then correct our course with the right coordinates," said Anna.

"Aye, aye, Captain." Ravi gave a jokey salute.

"No rush, though, right? Don't we have time to stop for a few seconds and check out these zero crystals? I really want to see what they look like."

"I do too." Anna looked around for a place to stop. They'd been riding through a narrow valley that led them gradually upward. She brought the Cheetah to a halt beside a rock formation that rose in dark spires out of the snow.

Ravi reached behind the seats for the Talon. He laid it on his lap and very carefully slid open the lid. He peered in. Anna bent over and peered in too.

"Where are they?" she said.

"I don't know." Ravi tilted the box from side to side. "I don't see anything."

"It's possible they could be invisible to the naked eye," said Anna, but even to herself, she didn't sound convincing. "Hand me the box."

Ravi did. Anna took off one glove. "If they're so extremely cold, I should be able to feel them," she said. She poked around inside the box with one finger. It was cold in there, but no colder than everywhere else. She thought she'd feel something like tiny pebbles or grains of sand—but there was nothing.

"I don't get it," said Ravi. "You scraped that baby crawler really hard."

"I know. But maybe not hard enough." Her voice was grim. "We're going to have to find another one," she said. "We have to try again."

"I guess we do," Ravi said reluctantly. "Should we go back to the same one?"

"No. And not its mother either. She's already furious at us. We'll find a different one."

"Where?"

Anna shrugged. "We'll just drive until we see one. There must be more."

Ravi put away the Talon, and Anna started the engine. They drove on up the sloping valley. Black rocks rose on either side of them, and snow drifted down in scattered flurries. After several minutes, they came to a place where the valley opened up and they could see that they had arrived at the top of the slope. Spread out below them was a wide plain of low hills, and to the east, along the shore of what looked like an immense silver lake, the snowy ground was dotted with humped dark shapes huddled together. Immense whirlwinds of snow swirled among them. The snowflakes flew in a peculiar way, sideways and upward as well as down.

Anna stopped the Cheetah. They both stared out at the view.

"Ice crawlers," said Anna.

Ravi nodded, his eyes wide. "Hundreds of them," he said.

"And those whirlwinds," said Anna. "I don't think they're just wind."

"No," said Ravi. "Those flakes flying off them—they must be locusts."

15

Dash and Carly had made it into the cave. Compared to the outside, the cave was warm—that is, Dash thought, it was not quite cold enough to freeze off a person's face and send it in ice splinters crashing to the ground. They couldn't take off their snowsuits, of course, but they were out of the wind. Some distance away, the mother crawler was heading toward them, but she was no longer a danger. She was much too big to get into the cave.

Dash was breathless, and he felt almost too weak to stand. He sat still, leaning against the cave wall, and waited, not trying to speak or move. After a few minutes, when his breathing came more easily, he stood up, hoping he looked normal, steadying himself with a hand against the wall.

"Are you okay?" Carly asked, and he said he was. "Are you sure? You don't look too good."

"I'm sure." Dash stepped away from the wall. "Come on," he said. "Help me with TULIP. We need to get warmed up."

They set TULIP on a low ledge and huddled around her. They held out their hands to her glowing belly, but it was hard to get their whole selves warm at once. The blackness of the cave loomed around them. Dash imagined they must look like the cave dwellers of ancient times on Earth, small in the darkness, bending over one bright spot of fire.

Dash knew that there had been ice ages on Earth. Could those times return? Would the people of Earth someday be living in caves again, crouching around fires? He shivered and inched closer to TULIP. He felt the darkness of the cave darkening his thoughts. There was not one of the planets they had visited that he would have wanted to live on. Not tropical J-16 with its ravenous reptiles, not mechanical Meta Prime, not ocean-covered Aqua Gen, not stony Infinity (although he wouldn't mind having one of those flying horses), and certainly not frozen Tundra. He felt a moment of sharp homesickness and sighed.

Carly picked up on the sound. "What was that about?"

Dash pushed away his dark thoughts. "Just wondering where the warm beaches are on this planet," he said. "And the palm trees."

"And the swimming pools," said Carly, smiling. "And the hot dogs."

The light moment felt good, but it was brief.

They were cold, and not happy. They had not yet succeeded in their mission. Anna and Ravi had the zero crystals, but they did not. And with the Streak broken, it wasn't clear how they'd get them. It was starting to feel like Aqua Gen all over again. A broken vehicle. No way to get the element without it . . .

Carly sat next to TULIP, with her arms around her bent legs and her chin on her knees, thinking. Dash lay on his back with his boots against TULIP's middle. After a while, he felt his mind begin to start warming up again. "I have an idea," he said.

"Good," said Carly, raising her head. "What is it?"

"We need those zero crystals," said Dash.

"Right," said Carly.

"And we can get them only from an ice crawler."

"Right," said Carly.

"But," Dash went on, "we don't have much in the way of transportation. We could go for maybe ten minutes in our broken snowmobile without more or less freezing to death. So really we have just one course of action."

"I know what you're going to say." Carly didn't sound happy about it. "We have an ice crawler coming right toward us. How convenient."

"That's right," said Dash. "We have to get the crystals from her."

"But she's angry. And she's dangerous."

"What choice do we have? Once we get the crystals, we won't need the Streak anymore. We can call Chris to come and get us, and we'll be out of here."

"So," said Carly, "your plan is that we should walk up to the ice crawler and use the Talon on her while she tries to eat us or crush us to death."

"No," said Dash. "My plan is much better than that. We want that crawler to come right up to us. She's way too big to get into the cave. But we want her to *try* to get in. To press some part of her huge front end against the entrance so that we just step up close, scrape her with the Talon, and get our crystals."

"And after that, she goes away?"

"Sooner or later, yes," said Dash.

Carly inched a little closer to TULIP and thought about this. "I see one flaw in this plan," she said.

"Which is?"

"Why would the crawler *want* to get into the cave? We don't really know if she's interested in eating us. As far as we know, crawlers eat only locusts."

"Exactly," said Dash. "And that's what we'll offer her."

He went to the entry of the cave. "Look," he said, pointing outward. "There she is, coming toward us. At that rate, she'll be here in maybe six or seven minutes. So we have to work fast." He stepped outside, motioning for Carly to come with him, and he tromped through the snow to the Streak and reached inside—easy to do, since the top was no longer there. He bent over, as much as his bulky suit would allow him to, and when he stood up again, he had an armful of dead snow locusts.

"We'll scoop out as many as we can," he said, "and spread them around outside the cave and a little way inside."

"Gotcha," said Carly. "We're laying bait. Let's do it."

From the back of the Streak, Dash took a lightweight metallic capsule that held a cable that was part of standard expedition equipment. He opened the capsule, put the cable aside, and used half of the capsule to scoop up locusts. Carly took the other half from him and used it to spread the locusts around, making a locust carpet outside the cave and partway in. They moved as fast as they could, glancing up every few seconds to see how close the ice crawler was.

The last time they looked up, she was about a hundred feet away.

"Okay," cried Dash, "let's get inside!"

They stood just within the cave entrance and watched the crawler approaching. She came slowly across the snowy ground and started up the slope toward the cave.

Dash took the Talon from his pack and held it up. Its two sharp points glittered in the light. "Do you want to do it? Or shall I?"

"You do it," said Carly. "I'll hold the light."

The crawler came steadily toward them, its pale skin making it almost invisible against the snowy ground. Dash couldn't help wondering if it was leaving a slimy trail behind it, like a snail. It made no sound, but every now and then, it reared up and its gray underside was like a mammoth column suddenly rising from the ground. Dash could see its dark mouth opening and closing.

Thirty feet away. Twenty feet.

Dash held the Talon in a tight grip, ready to strike as soon as the crawler came up to the cave. His heart was hammering, but he felt confident. They had a good plan, and their mission here was almost over.

Then came a sound from somewhere in the distance. It was a long, desolate moo.

The crawler stopped.

The moo came again.

Carly peeked out of the cave. She scanned the vast white landscape.

"It's the calf," she said. It was maybe half a mile away, all by itself at the base of a hill. It was crying.

The big crawler slowed, stopped, and changed course. It made a huge U-turn and headed away from the cave. Dash saw his plan fall apart.

"We'll go after it," said Carly. "We have to. It's our only chance."

Dash nodded. "In the Streak," he said. "We'll freeze, but it won't take us long. We should probably leave TULIP here so we'll be less noticeable."

"Good call. I think they can sense heat," said Carly.

So they jumped in, Carly at the wheel. She revved the engine, and they took off, following the crawler, going just fast enough to catch up with her but not—they hoped—fast enough to scare her into attacking them again.

"Pull up alongside," said Dash, "and try to get close enough so I can reach."

For a minute, the Streak and the crawler glided over the snow side by side. The crawler's pale side towered next to the little snowmobile like a wall.

"Closer," said Dash. He stood up and leaned from the Streak, stretching the Talon out toward the crawler's side.

Carly pulled in closer.

Dash leaned, reached—and miscalculated the distance. He toppled from the Streak, bumping against the crawler as he fell. The crawler's sides bulged and rippled. It reared up, its massive bulk looming over Dash like a skyscraper.

Lying on his back in the snow, Dash saw its gray underside rise over him and its mouth open into a black cavern, rimmed with teeth. From deep within the creature came a hissing noise, like a ton of sand rushing down a metal slide.

"Carly!" Dash screamed. "Catch!" He flung the Talon to her with all his might. Then he curled himself into a ball and rolled, and when the crawler crashed back down to land, Dash was not underneath it.

With one hand, Carly steered the Streak, driving right next to the crawler's back end, just inches away, and with the other hand, she gripped the Talon and drew it down in a long line on the slick skin. She did it as gently as she could, considering the tricky situation. The Talon left a stripe like a tiny railroad track.

"Got it!" she screamed. "Come on!"

Dash scrambled to his feet, Carly swooped the Streak up beside him, he climbed in, and in moments, they were back to the cave. They tumbled out, weak in the knees, panting, freezing, and laughing. Carly held up the Talon, and with what breath they had, they both cheered.

"Now back inside!" Dash said. "Back to our pal TULIP! Let's get warm!"

16

Anna and Ravi hadn't moved yet from their spot on the cliff. They couldn't take their eyes from the vast, unnerving view before them: the great gathering of ice crawlers on the slopes of the low hills, the whirlwinds twisting and towering among them, and the strange silver lake, whose waters also appeared to be in motion.

"We have to make a plan," said Anna.

"That's right," said Ravi. He gazed at the sight before him with awe. In a way, it was beautiful, almost like an old-fashioned photograph—black, white, gray, and silver. But he wasn't eager to go down and get into that scene himself.

"We'll find one of those beasts that's kind of apart from the rest, a straggler." She pointed downward.

"See? There's one. And there's another one, over by that lake. We'll pick that one. We have to move up on it fast, do the job, and get away."

"As long as it doesn't have a calf next to it," said Ravi.

"Right. And we'll have to steer clear of those whirlwinds of locusts." Anna's voice turned businesslike. "You do the driving this time," she said. "Get us up close to the one by the lake. I'll be ready with the Talon."

They swapped places, and Ravi started the motor and guided the Cheetah down the steep slope into the valley. The way was rough. He had to keep a sharp lookout for rocks that could scrape or break the Cheetah's runners, and for patches of slick ice where the Cheetah could slide sideways, tip, and tumble downhill. He was so focused on all this that he was taken by surprise when the ground leveled out, and he looked up to see two of the huge, blubbery creatures only a short distance ahead.

But he had no time to sit and look.

"On your left!" Anna cried out, and when Ravi looked left, he saw the white finger of a whirlwind bearing down on them, so close that a few stray locusts were already batting against the windshield.

He steered hard away from it, only to see another one just ahead.

"Go right!" Anna yelled, and he did, and they passed the twisting spiral just as it dissolved, releasing a blizzard of locusts, cutting off their view completely.

"Slow down!" Anna yelled.

"I know, I know!" Ravi yelled back. "I have to, I can't see!"

Out of the whiteness loomed a huge dim shape. Ravi had to swerve fast to miss it.

"That's our crawler!" cried Anna.

But right away, they could see that it wasn't the isolated one they'd been aiming for. Other crawlers clustered near it at the top of a slope, at least ten or fifteen of them. As the storm of locusts passed over them, they reared up, opening their mouths, and then they curled into enormous balls and rolled downhill.

"Left, left!" screamed Anna, and Ravi curved left, and then right and then left again, dodging the moving boulders and the spirals of wind, and it went that way for what seemed like ages until Anna pointed to the right and shouted, "There! That's the shore of the lake, and there's that one crawler by itself."

They'd come into the clear somewhat. Only a couple of spirals twisted nearby, and the air was free of flying locusts. The lone crawler must have eaten all it wanted; it lay still on a bank of ice. Beyond it was a lake like no other Ravi and Anna had ever seen.

"How can there be a lake on a planet where the temperature is way, way below freezing?" Ravi said. "If it's a lake, it should be frozen."

"But it isn't frozen," said Anna. "It's moving."

And yet it wasn't moving the way water moves. There were no waves coming in toward the shore. There were no ripples caused by the wind. Instead, it looked as if the lake was being stirred by an enormous, invisible spoon. Its water moved in a circle, slowly.

"And it isn't water," said Ravi. "It has to be some other kind of liquid, something that doesn't freeze at the usual freezing point."

"It looks like mercury," Anna said.

Ravi agreed. What filled that lake looked thicker than water, and silver, not clear. At the edges, where the liquid swept up against the land, it broke here and there not into streams and trickles but into sprays of tiny silver balls that ran up the slope of ice and then rolled back down, where they melted into the lake again. Ravi couldn't stop watching. He felt a strong temptation to run over and catch some of those silver balls and hold them in his hand.

"Come on," Anna said. "We have to get the crystals."

"I just want to try one thing," said Ravi. "Wait, okay?"

He opened the Cheetah door and stepped out into the cold. With the toe of his boot, he kicked at a chunk of ice until it broke into pieces, and then he picked up a piece about the size of a tennis ball and pitched it into the lake.

Just as he'd hoped, the splash flew up in loopy metallic shapes and gleaming, wobbling balls.

But something else happened that he hadn't expected. The slow swirl of the lake quickened a little, as if the invisible spoon were stirring a bit faster. Interesting, he thought.

"Ravi!" Anna called through the radio. "Get back in here! We don't have time to play around."

Ravi climbed back into the Cheetah. "That wasn't playing around," he objected. "That was a scientific experiment."

"Use your science talent another way," said Anna, starting up the motor. "I want *you* to scratch the crawler this time."

"Okay." Ravi was glad to have the chance. Somehow Anna had done it wrong before. He thought she'd come down too hard with the Talon. He would do it more lightly. After all, Colin had told them the crystals were right under the skin. Maybe they needed more precision here.

Anna drove the Cheetah cautiously toward the crawler, approaching it from behind, moving so slowly that the engine barely made a sound.

The crawler didn't move, except for a slight shudder of its bulging sides.

"Do you think it's asleep?" Ravi said. "In that coma that comes after they eat?"

"Probably," Anna answered. "I think it's safe to get pretty close." She drove along the icy shore of the lake. Flecks of snow and stray locusts sprinkled the windshield, driven sideways by the wind, which seemed to be getting stronger.

When they were about ten feet to one side of the crawler's back end, Anna brought the Cheetah to a halt. "Are you ready?"

Ravi turned around and pulled the Talon from behind the seat. He took a good look at the crawler, which still hadn't moved. He visualized his plan of attack: run up fast, do the scratch, and run like crazy back to the Cheetah.

"Ready," he said, and jumped out.

The first part of his plan worked perfectly. He ran right up next to the crawler, raised the Talon, and brought it down along the creature's flank, very lightly, making a faint pink stripe against the skin.

He was turning back toward the Cheetah when Anna called to him over the tech, "Harder! Do it harder!"

He didn't see why—she'd already tried a hard scratch and it hadn't worked out very well—but she was the commander, and so he obeyed. He brought the Talon down hard.

And that was when his plan went terribly wrong. The ice crawler came out of its sleep. It didn't make a sound, but it gave a titanic twitch. Its whole massive body crimped in the middle, and the rear

part of it swept sideways, struck the Cheetah with terrific force, and flung it—and Anna—into the lake.

Ravi heard Anna's horrified scream as she sailed through the air, and he saw the Cheetah splash down. He waited in terror for the lake to engulf it, but the Cheetah, with Anna still inside, didn't sink. The liquid in the lake swirled faster and faster, around and around, growing deeper in the middle, like a funnel. It carried the Cheetah and Anna around with it, as if it were trying to swallow them.

Ravi grabbed his radio transmitter and punched in the Alpha team's frequency. "Emergency!" he yelled. "Extreme emergency!"

Anna tried her best to keep panic at bay. She screamed only once, when the Cheetah went flying from solid ground into the air and then plunged into this terrible metallic water. The impact banged her sideways against the door and then back against the seat. It jolted her hands from the steering wheel. For a moment, all light was gone because the Cheetah had flipped upside down, but it righted itself and steely light flooded in again.

When she found that she was still alive, and that

the Cheetah was riding the current rather than going under, Anna forced herself to stop shaking and to breathe. From the window she could see nothing but swirling silver—above her, rising almost vertically, and far below her, narrowing and darkening. She was inside an immense funnel, being carried around its inner surface. The shore was just a narrow white curve high above her; the sky looked miles overhead.

She tried her two-way radio: "Ravi! Ravi! Can you hear me?"

An answer came, but the words were broken and blurry.

She tried again, her voice rising: "Ravi! Help me! Call for help!"

His voice came again, still blurry, but she made out the words: "Yes, getting help. Hold on!"

She knew he was trying. He would be calling the Alpha team—what else could he do? She didn't like asking for help from them. But at this point, she knew, it was way too late for pride.

Rocking gently, the Cheetah circled the funnel. It didn't take Anna long to realize that each time around, she was being carried a little farther down into the whirlpool.

17

Piper sat in her air chair next to one of the training room's treadmills. She had her eyes on the clock, watching the time. In a few minutes, she'd be out that door. It would be so easy, except of course that SUMI mustn't see her go. She had to figure out how to distract her. And the timing had to be just right.

She waited. Minutes passed, incredibly slowly. Finally it was twelve forty. Piper's heart began beating faster.

"SUMI," she said. "Want to play a new game?"

SUMI looked up. "New game?" she echoed.

"Yes. It's sort of like hide-and-seek, but different."

"Different," SUMI said.

"Right. And more fun! Here's how it works."

SUMI cocked her head, listening.

"It's called hide-and-squeak." Piper explained. "Person number one hides in the equipment closet." She pointed across the room, to the door of the closet that held balls, rackets, running shoes, weights, and spare machine parts. "Person number two has to hide this"—she held up a bright orange football—"in a place that's really hard to find. When it's hidden, person two makes a squeak like this." In a high, sharp voice, Piper squeaked. "Then person one comes out and has one minute to find it."

"Who is person one?" said SUMI. "Who is person two?"

"I'll be person one the first time," Piper said. "I'll go in the closet. You hide the football and squeak when you're ready."

"Good game," said SUMI.

Piper handed her the football, which she clutched between her skinny arms. Then Piper floated across the room, opened the door of the closet, and went inside. She closed herself in. Now she just had to hope that SUMI would hide the football quickly.

It took her about two minutes. A high, metallic squeak sounded, and Piper came out of the closet.

"Where could it be?" she said, looking around in a puzzled way. She floated this way and that, searching for the bright orange of the football. It had to be down near the floor, since SUMI was too short to reach high up. Where could she have put it? She looked behind the bank of servers, behind the controls console, behind the weight-lifting bench. She didn't see it.

"Eighteen seconds left," said SUMI.

Piper zoomed down closer to ground level and circled the room.

"Four seconds left," said SUMI.

"I see it!" cried Piper. "Right there!" It was a clever hiding place: on the floor beside the closet, where it would be out of sight behind the door when Piper opened it. "I win!"

"You win," said SUMI in a gloomy voice.

"Your turn," Piper said. "You go in the closet, and I'll hide the football."

"This time I will win," SUMI said.

"Remember, you have to wait until I squeak."

SUMI shuffled into the closet, and Piper closed the door. Then, working in complete silence, she bent down from her chair and grasped one of the rolled-up yoga mats that stood against the wall. She pulled it in front of the closet door and went back for another mat, and then another. It would have been much better to roll one of the big exercise machines to block the door, but there was no way she could manage that. The mats would have to do. She did manage to lean a couple of five-pound weights against them.

I'm sorry, SUMI, she said silently. *I'm sure someone will let you out soon.*

Then she sped to the console, entered the code, and opened the training room door. For a second, she hovered, listening, and when she heard no voices and no footsteps, she flew out. She heard the door lock behind her.

She was free, free! She was going home at last!

The *Light Blade*'s main corridor was empty. Piper looked both ways. No sign of anyone, and no sound. She flew out of the training room and closed the door silently behind her. Someone would find SUMI sooner or later; being locked in the supply closet for a while wouldn't hurt her.

Now Piper had to move quickly. It was twelve fifty-five. The engine room should be in the same place where it was on the *Cloud Leopard*—straight down the hallway. An easy flight, if she could do it without being seen. She made her way past the door to the research lab—and then, up ahead, she saw someone pop out of a portal.

It was Niko. He tumbled out, did a quick somersault, and jumped to his feet. She had only a second to get out of sight. There was a door to her left. She hit the control panel and the door silently slid open. She saw only darkness inside, but she steered in anyhow and the door closed behind her. She would just wait here until she didn't hear Niko's footsteps any more.

Slowly, a dim light began to shine—there must be a sensor in here that detected a person's presence. She was in a supply closet, Piper saw. Stacks of boxes held lightbulbs, coils of cable, and electronic equipment, and there was a clothes rod with spare space suits, thermal underwear, and a row of boots below. Surely Niko wouldn't be coming in here.

She waited and listened. She heard footsteps passing the door—two sets of footsteps. Someone else must have met up with Niko. They didn't pause, and the footsteps faded away. She waited another whole minute, and then she opened the door and peered out.

Empty corridor. Only a few dozen yards to the door of the engine room. She sailed to it, slid it open, and flew in.

18

Safe in the cave, Carly and Dash collapsed next to TULIP. Dash took a long breath. "You're sure you got the crystals?" he asked.

"I don't know," Carly said. "Let's find out."

While Dash held the flashlight, she slid open the lid of the Talon. They peered inside. The light glittered on something that looked at first like salt. It was a sprinkling of tiny crystals, each one clear as glass and perfectly spherical.

"We did it," Carly whispered.

"They're beautiful," said Dash. "And you can feel the cold coming from them."

It was true. The tiny crystals radiated a cold that almost felt like heat—a burning cold. They could feel it on their faces, searing their skin.

Carly closed the Talon and set it aside. She took off her pack and reached into it. "Good time to celebrate with a snack," she said, pulling out two small packets and handing one of them to Dash. She turned off her flashlight to keep the battery from running down, and they sat there in the dark, munching on chocolate-raspberry energy bars.

When they'd finished, Dash stood up. "I'll call Chris now and ask him to come and get us. I'll need to go out—probably won't be able to get a signal in the cave. Be right back."

Outside, snowflakes came at him hard, like tiny splinters of glass. Snow had fallen into the cab of the broken Streak, mounded on the seats, and made a white rim on the steering wheel. The Streak looked like an abandoned wreck.

Dash leaned against it. He'd been holding on to his last bit of strength, and now it threatened to drain out of him. He entered the number for the *Cloud Leopard* control on his transmitter. "Calling Chris," he said. "Alpha team calling, ready for pickup."

But there was interference on the line. A loud crackling sounded in his ear, and a panicked voice came through. It wasn't Chris. It was Ravi, shouting so fast and desperately he could barely understand what he was saying.

"Ravi, slow down!" Dash shouted. "What's happening?"

In the rush of words that came back, Dash made out just a few: *lake, Anna, drown,* and *die.*

"Say it again!" he called. "I didn't understand!"

This time Ravi spoke the words loudly, clearly, and with space in between. "Anna . . . and . . . Cheetah . . . thrown in LAKE. She could . . . DIE. COME RIGHT NOW!"

Dash still didn't understand—a *lake?*—but he got the main message. The Omega team needed rescuing. "Coming!" he shouted. "As fast as we can! Coordinates, Ravi!"

Ravi sent them, and Dash entered them in his MTB, and then he made a quick call to Chris. "Ignore my previous message. We're not ready for pickup," he said. "Emergency."

"What? What do you mean, emerg—" Chris said, but Dash cut him off. No time to talk now.

Carly had run out of the cave and was standing next to him, hopping with impatience. "What's going on? What happened to them?"

"I'm not sure," said Dash. "But Ravi sounded totally serious. Anna fell in a lake, I think."

"How do we know this isn't another trap?" Carly asked.

Dash shrugged. "I guess we don't. But we're the kind of team that helps when someone's in trouble. So we need to check it out. We'll just have to be careful."

"Yeah, okay," said Carly. Both of them looked at the snow-covered Streak. "It's not like it doesn't run."

Dash agreed. "It's just that we'll freeze to death riding in it without the roof."

"We'll have to take turns driving," Carly said. She got to work, brushing the snow off the seats and the dashboard. "I'll go first. While I'm driving, you crouch down behind the seats with TULIP. Put the blanket over both of you. When I get so cold I can't go on, we'll trade."

"Sounds good," said Dash. His weariness vanished. Nothing like an emergency to jolt a person into action. He loaded TULIP into the Streak, and he and Carly dug around the runners to free them from the snowbank. Carly plugged the coordinates into her MTB and jumped into the driver's

seat, and Dash climbed into the back and hoisted the thermal blanket over himself and TULIP like a tent.

"Ready," he called, and Carly started the motor.

Though they went at top speed, stopping only to change places when one of them got too cold, it took Carly and Dash nearly fifteen minutes to reach the cliff from which they could see the herd of ice crawlers moving slowly around a range of low hills, creeping up slopes where locusts swarmed, curling up, and rolling down. Around them, high white cyclones of snow locusts formed, whirled, and dissolved. To the east was the strange, swirling lake. Its waters looked like pure liquid silver.

"There's Ravi," said Dash, who was driving. He pointed at a dark spot by the lake shore. And in the lake, he saw another dark spot, riding with the current, around and around and around. "And there—look, Carly! The Cheetah. With Anna inside."

Carly peeked out from under the blanket. "It's a giant whirlpool! She must be terrified. How will we ever get her out of there?"

"We'll find a way." Dash gunned the Streak, and they sped down the slope.

Piper slipped through the engine room door. The room was huge, bigger than a football field. Stacks of crates full of supplies were stored here, along with tarp-covered vehicles and other equipment to be used on the different planets. The light was dim, and the ceiling was very high. There was a smell of motor oil and the constant low roar of the machinery that made the *Light Blade* run.

Piper saw that the *Light Blade*'s transport ship, the *Clipper*, was parked near the docking bay doors. That worried her a little. Would there be room for the *Cloud Cat* to come in? She flew closer to the little transport ship and scoped out the space. It would be okay, she thought—just might need some careful maneuvering.

She checked her mobile tech. She had two minutes to find the switch that opened the outer door of the docking bay so that Gabriel could fly in. That shouldn't be hard.

Piper made her way around the edge of the room, past a tower of fuel packs, a row of recycling bins for parts they might be able to repurpose, and some piece of complicated equipment she didn't recognize. She felt along the wall where the switch should be, and there it was, just a little lower than the one in the *Cloud Leopard*.

She checked the time again. He should be here any moment. She flew to the rear window and hovered there, waiting. Her heart thrummed with excitement.

That was when she heard the pop and thud sounds of someone coming through a portal. Uh-oh. She floated quietly to the top of the tower of fuel packs and peeked over.

It was Colin. He walked toward the *Clipper*, putting on a helmet as he went. He opened the door of the cockpit and climbed in.

A shock went through Piper. Colin must be going to pick up the crew on Tundra! This would ruin everything! According to the plan, Gabriel should be out there in the *Cloud Cat* any second, and if Colin took off now, the two would meet head-on.

There was no time to wonder what might happen then, because it was happening as she watched. The door slid up, the *Clipper* rolled into the bay, the door slid down. She heard the outer door going up, coming down. She waited a minute, then another minute—and then she sped to the window and looked out. There was the *Clipper*, heading down toward Tundra. The *Cloud Cat* was nowhere in sight.

Gabriel, standing next to the *Cloud Cat*, checked his MTB. Time to open the inner door of the docking bay. He flipped the switch on the wall just to the right of it, and the door slid upward from the bottom, rumbling and clanking.

All right. Now to fire up the ship, roll it through the inner door, close the inner door behind him, open the outer door—and off to the rescue!

He climbed the short ladder to the cockpit and settled himself in the pilot's seat. He strapped himself in; he put on his helmet. The control panel, sensing his presence, flashed a yellow light. Okay. Now the prep routine—setting coordinates, making sure gauges were at correct levels, activating readouts. Gabe pressed buttons and swiped touch screens, his eyes focused on the task.

He estimated that it would take less than four minutes to travel to where the *Light Blade* was stationed. He had told Piper to open the outer door at exactly thirteen hundred hours. By now, she would have escaped from the training room, and so, since she was away from SUMI, he would have no way to communicate with her. Everything depended on their timing.

There. Finished and ready. He looked up—

Straight into the eyes of Chris, who was standing beside the cockpit window, looking at him with a big question on his face. "What's going on?"

Gabriel opened the door. "I'm going to pick up Piper."

"No way!" said Chris. "Not *now*! I need this machine to go get Carly and Dash from Tundra. They just called. There's some kind of emergency."

"Chris, I have it all planned!" Gabriel objected. "It will take twenty minutes, maybe less. It's critical!"

"Not as critical as getting the team. I don't know what's going on, but it could easily be a life-or-death situation."

"But Piper is waiting—" Gabe began.

Chris shook his head firmly. "I'm sorry," he said. "But she's been waiting for weeks. Another hour or so won't matter. Come on, Gabe. Be reasonable."

Reluctantly, Gabe climbed down from the cockpit and Chris took his place. "But we're going for Piper the instant you get back!" Gabe called up to him.

"Right," said Chris, strapping himself in.

Gabriel watched as the *Cloud Cat* rolled through the inner door, and then he turned and pitched himself into the nearest portal. There was a slight chance that Piper hadn't yet left the training room. He had to try to reach her and tell her to stay there a while longer. Otherwise, she'd be hanging out in the *Light Blade*'s engine room, counting down to the moment she'd open the docking doors. And when she did, he wouldn't be there. He didn't want that to happen.

In the training room, he ran for STEAM's console. He entered the connection code and the code that would put SUMI into sleep mode. Then he spoke into the transmitter. "Petunia! Are you there?"

He waited. No answer. "Petunia! Speed Devil Supreme calling! Please respond!"

Again—nothing but silence. He was too late. Piper had escaped her captivity, and unless something had gone wrong, she was waiting for him in the engine room. And he was about to let her down.

19

Ravi ran up to Dash and Carly as they coasted to a stop. "Quick!" he shouted. "She's getting pulled farther and farther down! What can we do?"

Dash got out of the Streak. He had been thinking about this very question as he drove down to the plain. It wasn't hard to zero in on a solution, since as far as he could tell, there *was* only one solution. "Somehow," he said, "we have to throw a line to Anna, have her attach it to the Cheetah, and then haul her out—without dumping her into the lake in the process."

"R-r-r-right," Ravi said. He was so cold that his whole body was shaking and his skin was deathly pale.

"Is her radio still working?" Dash asked.

"Off and on," said Ravi. "I know she's alive—that's all. And I radioed Colin to come. He might be able to help."

There was no time to talk about how this had happened. Dash figured it might have something to do with the enormous crawler that was gliding away from them, moving swiftly for a beast of its size. All the crawlers, in fact, seemed to be moving away from the lake, probably scared by the alien beings that had come among them.

Dash shouted into his radio, "Carly—we need the rope!"

Carly, warm from her time with TULIP, moved fast. She hopped out of the Streak, opened the back hatch, and rummaged around until she found the coil of rope that was part of their equipment. She carried it out to Dash and Ravi. "I don't know if this will be long enough. She's pretty far out there."

"We had a rope too," Ravi said sadly, "but it's on the Cheetah."

Dash took a moment to assess the problem. It wouldn't be easy to cast the rope far enough. Impossible, in fact; they'd have to tie a weight to the end. And their timing would have to be exact, because they were aiming for a moving target. And Anna would need to figure out the plan, or her radio would need to be working well enough for them to explain it.

And the Streak would need to have the power to pull her out.

And they'd all have to survive the bone-cracking cold for however long this rescue effort was going to take.

A lot of tough requirements.

"Carly," he said, "find a rock, about this big, long and narrow." He put his hands about six inches apart. "Ravi, get in the Streak behind the seats— TULIP's back there. Stay close to her and warm up. I'm going to drive right to the shore."

Dash could see that the power of the lake's circular current was going to be hard to pull against. He would need to give the Streak as much help as he could. He drove slowly along the edge of the lake. The shore was icy and sloped steeply down to the silver liquid. If he parked the Streak on the slope and roped the rear end of it to the Omega racer, it would be pulled backward into the vortex. He needed something to brace the rear of the Streak against—a solid snowbank would help.

Up ahead, Carly beckoned. Dash steered the Streak toward her, and she ran up to him. "Look." She held up the stone she'd found—it was just the right size, black and heavy and with a rough texture. "And over there"—she pointed—"is a ridge of ice that we could back up against."

Dash drove toward it. He looked out over the lake—the Cheetah was on the far side of the funnel now, moving slowly back toward them, a long way below ground level. He could just barely make out Anna's face in the window.

Dash brought the Streak to a halt. Ravi, who had stopped shaking quite so badly, climbed out. Carly was already busy tying the end of the rope to the back of the Streak.

"Here's how I think we should do this," Dash said. "First we have to tell Anna to get in the back part of the Cheetah, open the hatch, and get ready to catch the line."

"But what if the lake pours in when she opens the hatch?" Carly said.

"She'll have to try to balance the snowmobile so it stays on the surface," Dash said. "If she can't, then I'm afraid she's lost."

"This is all my fault," said Ravi. "I should never have listened—"

"Forget it," said Dash. "Here's what we have to do. We wait until the current is bringing her close to us—till she's not quite right below us, but almost. Then we throw her the rope—I'll do that. She catches it; she ties it to the Cheetah and alerts us when she's done. The ice ridge in back of the Streak will keep it from getting jerked toward the lake when she ties on. Once we're connected, we go forward, pulling. Carly, you'll be in the driver's seat."

Carly nodded and climbed in.

"Ravi, try to tell Anna what we're doing. I'm going to get in position."

Dash went to the edge of the lake and gazed out. The Cheetah was moving toward him, being carried smoothly by the circling current. He raised the rock to shoulder height. He waited.

"Anna says okay," Ravi called. "I think she heard me, and she's ready to open the hatch."

When the Cheetah was close, Dash heaved the rock. The rope trailed through the air, the rock fell, a hand in a heavy glove reached from the hatch—but before she could grab on, the rock splashed and sank.

Dash hauled on the rope. "Help me, Ravi!" he called, and Ravi took hold, and they both pulled, reeling the rope back to shore. Dash took hold of the rock and prepared to throw again.

He and Ravi waited and watched as the Cheetah traveled around. When it approached, a little farther down this time, Dash waited a bit longer than he had before. Then he heaved the rock.

This time, two hands reached out from the hatch.

"She's got it!" cried Ravi. He waited, listening. Another minute or so. "She's tying on! She's ready!"

"Ready to go," Dash radioed to Carly, and Carly let up on the brake and moved the Streak slowly forward.

The rope tightened. Far below, the Cheetah pitched back and forth as it was tugged forward by the current and upward by the rope. After a minute, it settled in one place, stern slanting up.

"Slow and steady!" Dash called to Carly, and she pressed harder on the accelerator. The engine roared, but the runners skidded. They couldn't get a grip on the snowy ground. Carly was only managing to stay in one place.

"I can't move forward!" she called. "Too slick!"

"Keep pulling. Steady speed."

"It isn't going to work!" Ravi wailed. "We're going to lose her!"

"No, we're not," said Dash. "I have an idea." He was remembering what Carly had said when they first saw Tundra—that creatures here were adapted to live in the cold and wouldn't have much use for the fireplaces or hot tubs that Gabe was joking about. The idea that had just come to Dash was so wild and risky it didn't have much chance of working. Still, some chance was better than none. "Ravi," he said, "tell Anna to untie the rope from the Cheetah. She has to circle the vortex one more time."

"She won't like that," said Ravi.

"Tell her we'll throw the rope down again when she comes back around," said Dash. "It's the only way."

20

When Ravi told her to untie the rope from the Cheetah, Anna felt close to despair. "Don't give up on me!" she radioed. *"Please,* Ravi!*"*

"Not giving up!" Ravi's voice came through more strongly now. "New plan! Go one more time around, hook up again."

So, reluctantly, Anna pulled at the knot that held the rope to the Cheetah's rear hitch. Her fingers were clumsy in their thick gloves, and stiff from cold. And the knot was tight, because it was being tugged from the other end. It took all the strength she had to pull the heavy cords apart.

As soon as she did, the Cheetah lurched sickeningly, rocked from end to end, and nearly threw her out through the hatch. But she didn't lose her

grip, and the current swept the Cheetah onward, farther and farther from her rescuers. On the long trip around the lake, Anna felt terror more than anything, but swirling around the vortex also gave her time to think. About winning at all costs. Never worrying about who she hurt along the way—even on her own team. And about the Alpha team. And how quickly and readily the Alpha team had come to save her. Right now, it was hard to think of them as enemies.

The Cheetah took a sudden dip, and Anna lurched forward, ramming her hands against the dashboard. She cried out. She was truly frightened. What if the Alpha team couldn't rescue her? What if she was sucked down into the depths of this horrible lake and her life ended right here?

At least she would die a hero. But would she really? She'd always tried to do the right thing. A leader had to be hard. But had she been too hard? Leaving Piper on Aqua Gen—had that been a good decision?

She stared up at the silver liquid that spiraled above her. Now that *she* was the one in trouble, things looked a little different. The Cheetah plunged and pitched, Anna's thoughts swirled, and the combination made her feel more sick and confused than she ever had before.

A wave splashed against the Cheetah's windshield and broke into droplets like sprays of bullets. Anna flinched. *If I get out of here,* she vowed silently, *I promise to be better. I'll be kinder. I'll be stronger. Just please, Alphas, save me!*

When the rope went loose, Dash and Ravi hauled it up. Then Dash shouted directions into his transmitter. "Carly, come a little this direction." He gestured with both hands toward himself. "Go slow."

Carly steered slowly toward Dash. Behind the Streak, the rope slid off the ridge of ice and dragged along the ground.

"Ravi, get in the Streak—in the back with TULIP," Dash said.

Ravi hopped in, and Dash leapt into the seat and strapped himself in. "Now head that way," he said. He pointed to the ice crawler that still lay a short distance away, twitching slightly, at the edge of the lake.

"Really?" Carly said. "That's the one that heaved Anna into the lake."

"I know," said Dash. "I'm going to be really, really careful."

"And do what?"

Dash didn't answer. "Stop right here," he said when they were twenty feet or so from the crawler. He got out, went to the back of the Streak, and untied the rope from the hitch. Then he walked toward the crawler, dragging the rope behind him.

Sharp flecks of snow blew against his helmet, and his legs were almost refusing to move. But he was utterly focused now on his task. He didn't have enough extra energy even to feel the cold.

He slowed down when he got close to the crawler and tried to move as quietly as possible. He was approaching the beast from behind. Was it asleep? He couldn't tell.

Carly's voice came over the radio. "Dash—are you out of your mind?"

He didn't respond. He was working with the rope as he walked, tying it into a loop.

The crawler's side bulged out. Dash stopped but nothing else changed, so he kept going. He radioed to Ravi. "How close is the Cheetah?"

"Maybe two minutes away," Ravi said back.

"Get ready to throw the rope down," Dash said. "Let me know the moment she's near."

In one smooth motion, Dash pitched the rope loop toward the crawler's rear end. It landed on the snow close to the crawler's tail. This wasn't a move STEAM or Chris had prepared him for. He had years of Little League to thank for his aim. The crawler didn't move. So he darted forward.

Now everything had to happen fast. With one hand, Dash grabbed the rope. He plunged the other hand into the snow and burrowed beneath the crawler's T-shaped tail, which was, for a beast of the crawler's size, relatively small—around three times the size of an ordinary ship's anchor, but since it was made of flesh and not iron, not as heavy. He lifted it up gently so he could slip the rope around it, and he tightened the loop.

The crawler seemed not to feel a thing.

"Ready on this end!" Dash shouted to Ravi. And to Carly he called, "Come closer now—slowly—and get outside the Streak."

"Here she comes!" Ravi said. "I'm throwing the rope!"

All three of them held their breath.

"She's got it!" Ravi called.

The rope began to slide sideways across the snow. Anna would have to work at top speed to tie it to the Cheetah before it was torn from her hands.

"She's done it!" Ravi yelled, and at the same time, the rope went tight, the crawler noticed that its tail was being yanked, and its whole body jolted in shock.

This was the crucial moment. Dash shouted through his radio: "Carly! Get TULIP out here!"

Right away, Carly understood the plan. She spent half a second being dazzled by Dash's crazy brilliance, and then she hauled TULIP out of the Streak and rushed her over to where Dash stood behind the crawler.

"Get out of the way, Dash!" she cried. The crawler's tail was swishing from side to side, but because the rope was pulling on it, it couldn't go far. Dash stepped away from it, and Carly stood TULIP directly behind the crawler and shouted, "Heat, TULIP! Blast it out there!"

TULIP did. The crawler began to move. TULIP moved with it, following a few feet behind, sending out heat that to a person would have felt like comfortable warmth, but to the crawler felt like fire.

The crawler, it was clear, wanted nothing in the world but to get away from TULIP.

It moved fast, for a crawler. Its enormous strength pulled the rope taut. Ravi, looking down into the lake, saw the Cheetah tilt and rise, stern first, up the wall of the funnel, across the ridges of the circling current. He saw Anna inside, frantically holding on. "It's working!" he yelled. "Keep going!"

TULIP plodded forward. The crawler, shuddering, bulging in and out, and hissing like mad, hauled itself across the snow.

And the Cheetah crested the rim of the lake, bounced over a bump of ice, landed with a crunching sound, and kept going.

"Cut the rope!" Carly yelled.

Dash had his knife ready. He slashed through the rope, and the Cheetah came to a jittering halt.

Anna opened the door and fell out, her legs collapsing under her. She stared at the crawler humping off into the distance and at TULIP, toddling back toward the Streak. She gazed up at Dash, Carly, and Ravi. She was shivering so hard she could hardly speak, but she did manage to get two words out.

"Thanks, guys," she said.

21

Beside the silver lake on Tundra, both teams huddled in the Cheetah, waiting for pickup. Dash kept his eye on Anna. Gradually, her shivering stopped and she began to look like herself again.

"Anna," Dash said. "We have to talk about Piper."

Anna frowned. "Piper is safe with us."

"But she doesn't *belong* with you. She's on our team."

Anna said nothing, but she began shivering again.

"We saved your life!" Carly said. "You owe us, Anna."

Anna looked up. She began to speak, but then her gaze went to the window. "The *Clipper* is here," she said.

"About time," Ravi said. He'd called Colin at least an hour ago—what had taken him so long?

The transport ship glided down onto the snowy slopes, blowing away great clouds of locusts and causing the ice crawlers to bellow in terror. The ship glided to a stop. A hatch in the roof opened, and Colin's head, enclosed in a helmet, rose out of it. Ravi felt a blast of sound from the radio transmitter in his ear.

"Omega team! What in the world is going on?! I want to know from *you*, Ravi, why you reported your location *completely* inaccurately. I have wasted an hour looking for you, not to mention the fuel for *three* landings and takeoffs!"

Ravi winced. He hadn't meant to give Colin wrong directions. "I was kind of upset," he said. "Sorry."

"Sorry isn't going to cut it," Colin said. "Get in here, Omegas. We have some talking to do."

Ravi burned with resentment. He didn't like being yelled at. Who *wouldn't* have felt upset, after what he'd been through? Who wouldn't have made a mistake or two?

Anna didn't care much about whatever Colin

was going on about. She was too exhausted. She and Ravi both dragged themselves onto the *Clipper*. Once inside, Anna collapsed, but Ravi took a moment to turn and give the Alphas a wave and silent *thank you.*

"This isn't over. We need to discuss Piper as soon as we're back on our ships." Dash said.

Ravi gave a shrug as the ship's door closed.

"We won't enter Gamma Speed without her," Dash called.

Dash and Carly watched as the ship rose with a blast of fire that left wide black circles on the white land. When it was gone, Carly walked over to the Cheetah, which was lying on its side. She stuck her head in the window and looked around. She felt on the floor and under the seats and in the cargo space in back, and there it was.

"What are you doing?" Dash called to her.

"Looking for this," Carly said, and she held up the Omega team's Talon. "I thought it might be here."

"They *forgot* it?" said Dash. "Maybe this is our leverage to get Piper back. But . . . how could they forget?"

"I bet there's a good reason," Carly said. She slid

open the lid of the small box. She peered in. "Yep," she said. "Nothing's in there. They didn't get the crystals after all."

Above them, they heard the sound of the *Cloud Cat* coming in for a landing. It skidding along the icy surface and whirled partway around before stopping. They could see Chris inside, waving at them.

Carly climbed on, and Dash followed. He felt tired, now that the pressure was gone. He sank into his seat.

"Mission accomplished!" Carly said to Chris. "We got some unexpected curves thrown at us too." She gave Chris a quick outline of their adventures. Dash gazed out the window at the white landscape of Tundra falling away.

"You did well against major odds," Chris said, steering the craft toward the *Cloud Leopard.* "And we'll be facing another crucial task as soon as we . . ."

All of a sudden Dash couldn't focus on what Chris was saying. Energy drained out of him, and he saw darkness at the edges of his vision.

Carly's voice seemed to come from far away: ". . . get Piper back."

Dash bent over and rested his forehead on his

knees. The voices around him went on, growing fainter.

". . . a good plan . . ." Carly's voice.

Then Chris's voice: ". . . still a couple of problems to be worked out, but . . ."

And then nothingness.

Piper had been waiting for over an hour. She sat in her air chair on top of a high stack of crates in the *Light Blade* engine room. Gabriel hadn't shown up. What to do now? She didn't know. So she stayed where she was. *Something* had to happen.

And after a few minutes, it did. She heard the rumbling of the outer door of the docking bay. Instantly she was on the alert, her excitement level zooming. Gabriel had made it after all! *Finally!* She listened for the sound of the ship entering the bay. She heard the whine of the landing gear, the bump of the wheels.

She held her breath.

The outer door closed, leaving the ship between airless space and the atmosphere of the *Light Blade,* and then the inner door began to rise.

Rescue! Piper was about to swoop down and cry

out a glad greeting to Gabriel, but as she watched the ship roll in, she saw something that stopped her. This ship did not look like the *Cloud Cat*. This wasn't Gabe coming to her rescue. Of course not! She would have had to open the door if it had been Gabriel.

This was the *Light Blade*'s *Clipper,* piloted by Colin, bringing Anna and Ravi home from Tundra.

She froze. If she stayed exactly where she was and perfectly still, here on top of this tower of crates, they would be unlikely to see her. She switched off her air chair and watched, barely breathing, as the Omega team got out of the transport ship.

No one looked very happy. Anna seemed exhausted, and Colin seemed in a worse than usual mood. "I am *more* than disappointed," he said as Ravi and Anna unzipped themselves from their heavy suits and took off their boots and gloves. "This was not the performance I expected from you."

Anna and Ravi didn't answer. They put their gear away, and Colin led them out of the engine room. A few minutes later, Piper heard his voice over the ship's intercom: "Our team has returned. Niko and Siena, report to the navigation deck."

Something must have gone wrong, Piper thought.

Where was the big welcome that usually greeted a returning team? And what about the Alpha team? Were they all right?

But the immediate question was, What should she do now? If the Omega team was back, the Alpha team probably was too. That meant that Gabriel had definitely failed in his attempt to rescue her.

"Dash!" The voice spoke gently in his ear. "Dash, do you hear me?"

Dash opened his eyes. Wasn't he on the *Cloud Cat*? No . . . He was in the med room. He seemed to be lying on his back, and Chris was bending over him.

"I'm okay," Dash said. His voice came out sounding strange and shaky. "I'm . . . fine."

Chris helped Dash sit up. Then he gripped him by the shoulders. "Listen to me, Dash," he said. "You are in very bad shape. I'm going to give you a shot right now, and after that I want you to stay still for several minutes to get some strength back."

Dash nodded. He sat there, focusing his mind on his heartbeat, summoning what calm and strength he could. Chris gathered the equipment, took Dash's arm, and gave him the injection, and then he sat down next to him. "Just wait now," he said. "Don't even move."

Dash closed his eyes. His thoughts wandered back to that icy planet. He said, "Tundra is an awful place."

Chris nodded in agreement. "Tundra is a planet that's almost dead. The few life-forms it has are pretty low."

"No kidding," said Dash. "A buglike thing and a sluglike thing."

"Right," said Chris. "But it wasn't always that way. I found some clues during the time I spent there about how it might have been, in the distant past. Not much—just a few things."

"Like what?"

"Fossils," said Chris. "Mostly in the caves, but some in cliff rocks too. I found the imprints of paws on a cave floor, and the remains of bones. I found fossilized leaves. I'm sure that thousands of years ago, maybe millions, Tundra was full of life."

"And then what happened to it?"

Chris shrugged. "Things change. Its sun could have dimmed. Systems get out of balance."

Dash was silent for a moment, thinking. "*Our* planet is alive," he said.

"Yes," Chris said again. "Teeming with life. The kind of place you want to protect and treasure."

Images of Earth filled Dash's mind: flocks of birds rising from a lake, a tiger prowling through tall grass, a school of silver fish in an ocean wave. Bustling human cities. Dogs in parks, chasing balls. "I really want to make it back there," he said.

"Of course you do." Chris stood up, so Dash did too. "That's why," Chris went on, "we have to take very good care of you. How are you feeling now? Better?"

Dash said he was.

"Good. Because we have a change of plan. We have to get to our next stop immediately, which means we're going into Gamma Speed right now. I'm going to announce that to the crew. And we'll need to tell them why."

"You mean tell them about me?"

"Yes. I'll do it, if you'd rather not."

"No," said Dash, though his heart sank at the thought. "I'll tell them."

Chris gave a curt nod. He turned and left the room, and a minute or so later, his voice came over the ship's intercom. "Urgent announcement," he said. "All crew to meet in the training room. Be there in thirty seconds."

22

Dash was still moving slowly, so by the time he arrived in the training room, the others were already there. Gabriel looked surprised; Carly looked alarmed. Even Rocket had a sense that something important was about to happen. He sat very still by Gabriel's side, his ears alert and eyes wide. STEAM, who wasn't too good at picking up emotions, stood by a stack of hard drives, prepared as always to supply or store information.

"Dash, are you okay?" Carly gasped. "I was so scared when you passed out on Tundra."

"Florida boy couldn't take the cold, huh?" Gabriel smiled at his joke, but it was a weak smile. He was clearly rocked by seeing his leader in such bad shape.

Chris interrupted them before Dash had a chance to answer. "A few minutes from now," he said, "we will be entering Gamma Speed. I'll be contacting the *Light Blade* soon to let them know."

There was a gasp from Carly.

"No way!" Gabe cried. "You can't be serious! We have to rescue Piper before we're going anywhere."

Chris shook his head. "I know you weren't expecting this, but we have an emergency. We have to go immediately."

"And leave Piper *behind*?" Carly couldn't believe her ears.

"I know it's not easy," Chris said. "But a rescue operation would take time. We don't know where on the *Light Blade* she is. We'd have to contact her somehow to find out. We could lose several hours."

"So what?" said Gabe. "What's the rush?"

Chris shifted his gaze to Dash. "Your captain will explain."

Dash got up and faced his team. He supported himself with one hand on the back of a chair. For a moment, he couldn't speak. Feelings were boiling around in him. This was his team, the people who had trusted him—and he had lied to them. The lies had been for a good reason, but had it been worth it? Should Shawn have chosen someone else for the

Cloud Leopard leader? Now he had put everyone in danger, and he wouldn't blame them if they turned against him.

He took a slow, long breath. "There's something about me you don't know," he said. "I'm older than you are."

Carly and Gabe looked puzzled.

"Not a lot—just six months," Dash went on. "Somehow they got my age wrong when they were choosing which of us should go on this voyage."

"So?" said Gabriel. "I don't get it."

"Hold on," Dash said. "I'll explain. The problem is the technology this ship uses to get us through our voyage and back home in a year. It's hard on adults—their systems can't take it."

"So?" said Gabriel again. "You aren't one."

"But I will be," said Dash. "This technology defines an adult as anyone over fourteen."

There was silence. The team began to understand.

"I've been getting shots to slow my metabolism," Dash told them. "The shots are designed to give me four hundred days of healthy travel. But they aren't working as well as they used to. Plus, I only have so many shots—and so many days. Time is running out for me." He paused. He wanted to be very clear. "Our voyage will take roughly sixty-five more days. Which means I'll turn fourteen during our next Gamma jump."

His team—all two of them—took a short, sharp breath. Gabriel looked at him as if he were a stranger. Carly seemed stricken—he could see her eyes glistening with tears. STEAM muttered, "Emergency. Emergency. Emergency, yes sir," in a quiet, troubled voice. Even Rocket raised his eyes to Dash's, as if he understood.

Again, it was Gabriel who spoke. "What could happen to you?" he said, all joking gone from his voice.

Dash didn't want to say it, but he had to. "Worst case—I could die."

Silence.

"I know you must feel betrayed," Dash said. "I'm really sorry this has happened. Probably Shawn Phillips made a mistake, choosing me for this mission, and he should have—"

But Carly interrupted him. "*I* don't feel betrayed!" she cried. "It was the right thing, choosing you for our leader. I want you to live! We'll get you home, I promise!"

"We will," said Gabriel more quietly. He turned to Chris. "We will—won't we?"

"Yes, we will—but only if we step up our pace. We have another planet to visit, and we'll have very little time to spend there. That's why we need to leave now. Piper will be all right with the Omegas. We just don't have time—"

"Yes, we do!" Gabriel cried out. "It's all set up! I've contacted Piper. She was locked in their training room, but I got the code for the door, and she's out and waiting for us right this minute in the *Light Blade* docking bay!" He wasn't sure of this, to be honest. It had been almost two hours since he said he'd come for her. She might be still waiting. She might not.

Chris's face lit up. "Gabriel! You astonish me. You mean—"

"Yes!" cried Gabe. "It will take us ten minutes!" He turned to Dash. "What do you say, captain?"

Dash, still a little shaky, couldn't take in what Gabe was saying at first. "Wait—you contacted Piper?"

"*Yes*, I'm telling you!" Gabe said. "I did it through STEAM—took control of their SUMI robot."

"Brilliant!" said Dash. He felt his strength flooding back in. "Get on it, Gabe!"

Gabriel ran for the portal, but before he flung himself in, he turned around for a second and flashed a big grin at Chris. "Chris!" he said. "Special favor—you can come with me!" Then he was gone.

"All right," said Chris. "Rescue operation under way."

Chris and Carly both followed Gabe into the portal. Dash stayed on the navigation deck with Rocket, who bounded at his side barking joyfully.

Ship's log 2.8

[Alpha team member: Dash Conroy]

[Comm link: audio feed, Cloud Cat]

This is Dash Conroy. Commander Phillips, I'm patching this through urgently so you know what's happening.

Tundra mission accomplished. Before we enter Gamma Speed we are staging a rescue. Gabriel and Chris are preparing the Cloud Cat. I am too . . . compromised . . . to execute this part of the mission. But we are going to get Piper.

Failure is not an option.

[End of transmission]

23

Piper was ready to give up on Gabriel. She'd been waiting for two hours, sitting on the stack of crates. It was pretty clear that he wasn't coming. She closed her eyes and tried to concentrate. What to do? It seemed there were three possibilities:

- She could leave the engine room, let the Omega team know she'd escaped from her captivity, and hope they would agree it was time to free her.
- She could leave the engine room and hide somewhere on the *Light Blade,* while trying to find another way to contact the *Cloud Leopard.*
- She could stay here in the engine room, hiding.

Flying, she decided, would help her think. She took off from the stack of crates and flew some loops and swoops high up toward the ceiling, and sure enough, her thoughts did seem clearer. She knew that the last thing she wanted was to be imprisoned again with SUMI. Better to stay here in the engine room for a while longer. Surely her team would figure out some way to rescue her before they left for their next destination.

So—might as well have some fun while she waited. She zoomed around the edges of the whole huge space, made a few quick loops, and then put the air chair into a steep dive and landed lightly on the floor. To her right was a small enclosed room, probably the room Colin used for putting together the elements.

She peeked through the little window in the door. Yes, there they were, in a row on a counter, the tubes that held the elements they'd gathered so far. Among them, she knew, was the Pollen Slither extracted from the planet Aqua Gen. The Alpha team had missed that one. Should she go in and take it? She tried the door. Not locked. No one would know if she went in. Right now, she figured they were all gathered somewhere, talking about how things had gone on Tundra. She reached for the door handle.

From somewhere behind her came a clanking, scraping sound.

Piper's heart gave a jolt. Was someone in here with her? The noise came again. She turned around—and there was the slogger that the *Light Blade* team had collected from Meta Prime. It looked just like TULIP—almost, but not quite. What was different about it? Its shape was the same. Its rosy belly was the same, or maybe brighter. It was the sounds that were different. TULIP's sounds were chuckling, humming kinds of sounds. The slogger here sounded as if it had a cold. It was going *chuff-chuff,* a sort of coughing sound, and then snorting loudly. It seemed to be trembling too. Maybe there was something wrong with it.

The longer she watched, the more sure she was: this slogger was not well. Its chunky body was shaking hard, the various parts of it clattering against each other, and its belly was bright red and swollen. Piper could feel the heat from the slogger, though it was many yards away. It was tottering toward her, as if it knew it was sick and wanted help.

Piper took off. She hovered above the slogger and watched, with growing alarm, as the red belly swelled and swelled, and then as a bright red crack opened across it and molten metal, so fiery orange-red she could barely look at it, trickled out. The slogger stopped walking. All its lights went off. It sank toward the floor as the crack widened and the red trickle became a stream. Where the stream slid across the floor, the metal of the floor hissed and curled and shrank back.

And with a shock, Piper understood. The slogger's molten metal would eat a hole through the floor of the ship, and the ship would be destroyed.

24

The Omega team assembled on the navigation deck for the post-Tundra meeting. Colin faced them, scowling. "Your mission was a failure," he said. "You are failures. I want you to go down onto Tundra again and get what we came for."

Anna was stunned. Go down there *again*? But she clamped her teeth together and said nothing.

Ravi was not so restrained. He gave a yelp of protest.

Colin flashed him an angry look. "We're in this to win," he said. "Are you on board with that or not?"

"Of course we are," Anna said.

"I guess," said Ravi.

But to Siena, listening, it was clear that Anna and Ravi resented Colin's disapproval. True, they hadn't retrieved any zero crystals, and they'd come close to losing Anna. They'd made it back, though, and should have got some credit for that. But Colin did not spare them a single kind word. That was unfair. More than ever, Siena felt that the Omega team was not where she wanted to be.

She ventured an observation. "But don't we have to stay with the *Cloud Leopard*? What about the Gamma jump? And we don't have the Cheetah—"

Colin didn't let her finish. "We have Piper. That will keep the Alphas out of Gamma Speed. We'll return to the planet again in two hours," he said. "Rest, and then get ready."

Everyone turned away in silence. Anna ducked into a portal, and Ravi and Niko followed a moment later. Siena headed down the corridor, confused and upset. She needed some time to think. She walked slowly.

And then she heard someone calling her name, and when she looked up, she saw Piper speeding toward her in her air chair. Siena couldn't make sense of it. Piper had escaped from the training room?

"Siena!" Piper cried. "There's a fire in the engine room! The ship is in terrible danger!"

"What? A fire?"

"Yes! The slogger is melting down! It's burning through the floor!"

The slogger. Molten metal. Fire. Piper, flying free. Siena didn't stop to try to put it all together. She turned and ran, and as she ran she cried out at the top of her lungs: "Emergency! FIRE!"

Niko darted out from the rec room. "What's wrong?"

"Piper says there's a fire!" Siena cried.

"In the training room?"

"No, in the engine room, I think—I don't know!" cried Siena. She looked around, but Piper had vanished. "It doesn't matter. Hurry! We have to find everyone! Let's get to the navigation room and call on the intercom."

"But shouldn't we go and check the engine room?" Niko said. "Maybe Piper is wrong."

"But what if she's right?" Siena was breathing hard. "If she's right, there's no time to waste. I'll head for the flight deck. You check Colin's quarters."

"Okay." Niko ducked into the nearest tube portal and was whisked away.

Siena kept running, shouting as she went. "Anna! Ravi! Where are you? Emergency!"

No response.

When she got to the medic room, she tapped in the route to the navigation deck and flung herself into the tubes. Moments later, she popped out again and nearly banged into Anna, who was standing by the ship's controls, looking out the wide window.

"Anna!" cried Siena. "There's fire in the engine room!"

Anna turned and frowned at her. "What are you *talking* about? Calm down."

Siena tried to catch her breath. "The slogger," she gasped. "Spilling molten metal. Eating through the—"

The look on Anna's face changed to horror just as the ship's alarm started blaring.

The intercom crackled to life. It was Colin. "Fire!" he shouted, so loudly that his voice was harsh and blurred. "Anna—call the *Cloud Leopard* right now. Our ship is *going down!*"

25

The *Cloud Leopard's* docking bay, where Gabriel was getting ready for Piper's rescue mission, was a whirlwind of activity. ZRKs buzzed around the transport ship, doing a few last-minute touch-ups. Carly checked the landing gear, and Gabe and Chris put on their helmets and climbed into the cockpit.

Rocket bounded into the room excitedly. Carly reached down and pet his head. It was almost as if he knew that they were going to rescue Piper.

As he closed the *Cloud Cat* door, Gabe hesitated. He was a little worried. He hadn't told anyone that Piper didn't know her rescue was coming late. She might be in the *Light Blade* engine room waiting, or she might not. They might get to the *Light Blade* and discover its bay doors hadn't been opened. What they'd do then—he wasn't sure.

He'd have to deal with that if it happened.

Right now, it was time to go. Gabe opened the inner door of the bay, and the *Cloud Cat* moved forward.

In the *Cloud Leopard's* control room, Dash was about to prepare the ship for Gamma Speed. He set the coordinates; he flicked the button for the intership communication so that as soon as Gabe was back with Piper, he could tell the *Light Blade* to get ready too.

First, though, he'd check in with Shawn Phillips back on Earth and give him a quick briefing on their status. He opened the transmission channel, made the right adjustments, and spoke.

"*Cloud Leopard* calling Commander Phillips," he said. "Dash here, please come in."

He waited, listening to the silent reaches of space.

After several seconds, a faint crackling sounded, and then came the familiar voice. "Phillips here. Glad to hear from you, Dash. How's everything going?"

Dash took a breath, about to answer, but before he could speak, the intership line buzzed, and buzzed again, furiously.

He picked it up. *"Cloud Leopard,"* he said. "Hold a sec."

But words came at him in a great rush, so fast he could barely understand them.

"Slow down!" he said. "Who is this?"

Phillips's voice came through faintly from the other channel. "Dash? What's going on?"

From the intership com, the voice rose to a shriek. "Dash! Our ship is on fire! We had to evacuate! We're on the *Clipper,* coming your way!"

He realized who was speaking to him. "Anna," he said. "Calm down. What are you talking about?"

Dash hadn't closed the ship-to-Earth connection, so Commander Phillips's voice sounded again. "Dash! Where are you? What's happening?"

But to Dash his commander's voice sounded tiny. He was focusing hard on Anna now, trying to understand what she was telling him.

Her voice was rising. "There's a *fire!*" she cried. "In the engine room!"

"The engine room? This isn't another trick, is it?"

"No, no!" There was a sob in Anna's voice now. "We barely made it into the *Clipper*—there were flames all around. In a moment, the whole ship will be on fire! Can we come aboard the *Cloud Leopard*?"

It was the sob that convinced Dash. He whipped around and sent a few words to Commander Phillips, keeping his voice as calm as he could: "Problem here. Needs attention. Will call later."

"Dash, I need to know—" said Phillips, but Dash realized there was not a moment to spare, even for his commander. He radioed the team: "Emergency! Halt rescue operation! *Light Blade* in distress!"

Gabe's voice came back. "What?!"

"There's a fire on the *Light Blade*," Dash said. "Anna just called—they're all in the *Clipper*. They need to come here."

"All of them?" Gabe said. "Piper too?"

With a shock, Dash realized he didn't know. He shouted into the intercom: "Anna—where's Piper?"

The answer at first was silence, and then a heartbroken wail. "Oh, Dash! I don't know where she is! I forgot about her!"

Dash felt his voice rising, loud and piercing. "How *could* you, Anna? How could you *forget* her?"

Anna broke into tears—something no Alpha or Omega had ever seen her do. "We'll go back. We'll find her. We won't leave her, I promise!"

In his rush, Dash had still not closed the ship-to-Earth connection, so Commander Phillips heard what he and Anna said. He didn't hear it clearly, because they were shouting so fast and loudly and because their words were blurry with static. But he knew that something terrible must have happened. He spoke again into the transmitter. *"Answer me, Dash!"*

No answer came.

He tried again. "Dash! This is a direct order! Tell me what's happening!"

Nothing but the silence of space and the faint crackle of static.

Phillips leapt to his feet as if to take action. His team was in trouble! Then he just stood there, in the communications office of Alpha team headquarters, shaking and raging at his helplessness, light-years away from whatever was going on.

Gabriel threw the *Cloud Cat* into reverse and backed it up. He signaled for Carly to close the dock door, and he and Chris jumped down. All of them had heard

Dash's message. Carly raced to the small window in the engine room's wall. "Look!" she cried. "It's true—I see flames in the windows!"

Chris and Gabriel crowded behind her. Gabe took in a sharp breath. What he saw horrified him. "We have to go and get Piper," he said. "Right now."

"But Anna promised to go back for her," said Carly.

"I don't trust Anna," said Gabe. "Do you?"

Carly didn't answer.

Nearby, the *Clipper* hovered, as if Anna were hesitating. Beyond it, the *Light Blade* burned. Fire flickered in its rear windows.

"Piper is on that ship," said Gabe. "In that fire. How can we not try to rescue her?" He wanted to jump back onto the *Cloud Cat,* go full throttle, and snatch her out of danger.

But the truth of the situation was setting in. The *Light Blade* was being destroyed faster than they could get there. How could they possibly save Piper? How could anyone?

At that moment, Dash flew into the engine room, with a ZRK Commander right behind him. "We need to go—" he started to shout, but then he saw what everyone was looking at.

The flames licking in the windows crept through the seams of the *Light Blade*'s hull. The silver surface blackened and crumpled, and the *Light Blade* drifted, nose down. The Alpha team, usually so daring and quick-witted in extreme situations, looked on in complete shock. Silence.

This time, there was nothing they could do.

Find the Source. Save the World.

Follow the Voyagers to the next planet!

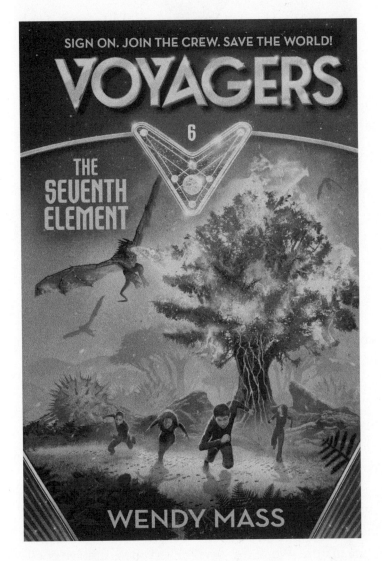

Chris wore his serious expression. "In order to have any chance of retrieving the element, you'll have to convince three different species to work with you. And trust me, that won't be easy."

After a few seconds of silence, Ravi said, "They're werewolves, aren't they?"

"They are not werewolves," Chris said.

Ravi pretended to look disappointed.

"I bet it's ghosts!" Siena said.

"Giant marshmallow men!" Gabriel shouted.

"Come on, guys," Anna said firmly. "Let Chris talk."

"Thank you, Anna," Chris said. But before he could say anything else, Anna said, "It's vampires, isn't it? Bloodsucking vampires?"

They all laughed again. Anna grinned.

Chris laid his head on the table. "So this is what having eight kids on board one spaceship is going to be like."

"Teenagers," Carly corrected him. "We're all thirteen now."

Before someone could point out that they'd celebrated everyone's thirteenth birthday during their voyage except his, Dash quickly jumped in. "Sorry, Chris. We'll try to be more mature. Won't we, guys?" Everyone grumbled good-naturedly, but agreed. "So what's so bad on this planet?" he asked.

"Well, you need to gather fresh Dragon Cinder," Chris explained. "That's going to require working with the various life-forms of the planet. First there are the elves, whose trust you will need to gain right away."

"Elves?" Ravi repeated.

"Yes," Chris answered. "You will need them as allies. Fortunately, their language is not that different from your own, so communicating with them won't require the use of your translator."

"That sounds like a cakewalk," Ravi said. "What else ya got?"

"Ogres," Chris said.

"Sweet!"

Everyone turned to look at Gabriel as though he'd lost his mind.

"What?" he said with a shrug. "That Shrek guy is cool, right?"

"Actually," Chris said, "ogres are terrible creatures. They attack the peaceful elves on a whim and will do anything to hoard as much silver and metal as they can. They are cruel, angry, and spiteful."

"They sound lovely," Piper said. "Let's steer clear of them, shall we?"

Chris shook his head. "Unfortunately, you will need them. They're the only ones who can lead you to the dragons."

Niko sat up straight. "Dude! Did you say *dragons*?"

Chris nodded. "That is the third and by far the fiercest creature you will encounter."

"Awesome!" Niko replied, high-fiving Gabriel and Ravi. "You were right, Siena!"

Chris looked puzzled. "Siena, you knew there'd be dragons?"

Siena nodded. "It's a gift I have, seeing the future."

"Interesting," Chris said, typing into his Mobile Tech. "That wasn't in your profile material. I'm going to have to speak to Shawn about being more thorough. Anyone else have a surprise talent they've kept hidden?"

"I'm kidding," Siena told Chris. "Of course I can't see the future. Niko_ has a thing for dragons, and we were talking about it one day, that's all."

"Oh," Chris said, clearly disappointed. He reached back over to his Mobile Tech and hit the delete key.

"Anything else we should know now about the mission?" Dash asked. He knew he wasn't going—he couldn't let his worsening condition put the others at risk. It was a big blow, but what choice did he have? He was trying to focus on their journey right now, not their destination. There would be plenty of time for that. Before Chris could answer, Dash added, "I'd really like to get everyone started with their new jobs on the ship."

Chris hesitated before answering. There was more he could tell them about his history with the elves. He looked around the table at the anxious faces staring back at him. He sighed. Why steal their last moments of relative safety?

Chris shook his head. "I'm done for now." The kids jumped up, like it was the end of the day at school and they were sprung. "One more thing," he said, ignoring the few groans he heard. "Here." He handed a Mobile Tech arm band to each of the Omegas. "We made extras for the Alpha team in case one was damaged on a mission. Now you should have them."

Dash stood back and watched everyone playing with their Mobile Techs. Chris joined him. "Time for your injection," he said quietly.

Dash glanced at the group. The members of the Alpha team were showing the Omegas some of the cooler things the Mobile Tech could do. He'd have to stop thinking of them as Alphas and Omegas now that they were one team. They needed a new name.

No one noticed Dash and Chris slip out of the room. Rocket followed at their heels as they headed toward Chris's quarters.

"Did you tell the newcomers yet about your age?" Chris asked.

Dash shook his head. "I'll tell them in a few days, I promise. Everything is new for them now; I don't want them to worry that the leader Shawn chose might not be able to lead them after all. Anna knows, though. She figured it out."

Chris nodded. "Not much gets by her. She was a powerful opponent, and now you will need her to be a powerful partner."

"I know."

Chris opened his door, and before Dash could react, an arm reached out, grabbed Chris by the shirt collar, yanked him inside, and shut the door.

Jeanne DuPrau is the *New York Times* bestselling author of the City of Ember books, which have been translated into multiple languages and are a time-honored staple in elementary school classrooms.

Visit her website at jeanneduprau.com.

NEXT DESTINATION:
DARGON

The Voyagers have made it to the last planet. The sixth planet will require some careful maneuvering through a world of elves, ogres, and dragons, but then they will have all six elements they need to make the Source and save the world. So why is there space in the Element Fuser for a seventh element?

MISSION BRIEFING

REPORT TO BASE 10

ATTENTION: AUTHORIZED PERSONNEL ONLY

The Voyagers are facing the most dangerous environment yet. We need all hands on deck to complete the appropriate recon work. Your participation is crucial. Report to headquarters immediately.

- PLAY space-age games
- CUSTOMIZE your ZRK Commander
- DISCOVER new stories
- LISTEN to the adventure unfold
- EXPLORE a whole universe of extras

LOG ON NOW AND START YOUR JOURNEY!